LATINO HERETICS

LATINO HERETICS

edited by
TONY DIAZ

NORMAL

Published by Fiction Collective Two with support given by the
English Department Unit for Contemporary Literature of
Illinois State University, and the Illinois Arts Council

Address all inquiries to: Fiction Collective Two, c/o Unit for
Contemporary Literature, Campus Box 4241, Illinois State
University, Normal, Illinois 61790-4241

Latino Heretics

ISBN: Paper, 1-57366-077-9

Library of Congress Cataloging-in-Publication Data
Latino heretics / edited by Tony Diaz.
     p. cm.
  ISBN 1-57366-077-9 (alk. paper)
  1. American fiction--Hispanic American authors. 2. Hispanic
Americans Fiction. I. Diaz, Tony, 1968-   .
PS647.H58L38   1999
813'.54080868--dc21   99-27403
                                             CIP

Cover Art & Design: Todd Michael Bushman
Book Design: Owen Williams
Produced and printed in the United States of America
Printed on recycled paper with soy ink

Illinois ARTS Council
AN AGENCY OF THE STATE OF ILLINOIS

This program is partially sponsored by a grant from the Illinois Arts Council

CONTENTS

Tony Diaz

Tony Diaz is author of the novel *The Aztec Love God*. He is also the founder of Nuestra Palabra: Latino/a Writers Having Their Say, based in Houston, Texas, and the 1998-99 Writer in Residence at the Center for Mexican American Studies at the University of Houston.

Introduction

"Here in these woods, I cry out, I speak out. I glory in speech. It is my task in life to bring the news to the world, to sketch out truths so the very gods will see we are not slouching toward Gomorrah, but are crawling from its gates. Language holds the key, my relative clause. Language is the marvel and the blessing. Language is the map of our mind and of our hearts."
—From *Islas Coloradas* by Omar Castañeda.

I was sitting in a Manhattan library when I first read Omar Castañeda's work.

Manhattan, Kansas that is. And it was the multi-cultural issue of the literary journal *Kenyon Review* subtitled "De Colores." I was then a young, good brown man studying the craft of fiction writing at Kansas State University when Castañeda's short story "On The Way Out" made its way into my imagination.

I remember putting the fat journal down, pressing the veins over my temples, shaking my head, and thinking, *"This* is Hispanic Heritage?"

It was not what the American Imagination had prepared me to expect from a Hispanic Writer.

His short story, that art, had conveyed to me an approach to Fiction that would melt the old borders of which all writers are preoccupied with not being occupied by. I had read into the mind of a Latino Heretic.

"It would be marvelous to have the ability to act passionately within any sphere, yet to have a strong enough deconstructionist mind to warp into another and live there, too, with passion. Mastery of the internal conventions of each sphere would allow one, theoretically, to write across spheres, to write a

tunnel between spheres, or to make worm holes with deconstructionist techniques."
—Omar Castañeda in an interview for the *Americas Review.*

Minority Fiction.
Creative Writing Programs.
Book-of-the-Month-Club.
Literary journals.
Units.
Literary Fiction.
Craft. Newtonian Fiction.

These words were shaping and being shaped by the way writing was being shaped as "On The Way Out" became a part of the short story collection *Remembering to Say 'Mouth' or 'Face'* which would win the 1993 Nilon Award for Minority Fiction sponsored by Fiction Collective Two.

And the institutions that shaped these terms, and which were shaped right back, would baptize me with a Master of Fine Arts degree in Creative Writing—Fiction from the University of Houston in 1994.

I had been lured from my birthplace on the South Side of Chicago because I wanted to become a writer. I had tuned into a gorgeous image cast into the American Imagination about the power of writing, about mastering fine art, about the Southwest. Of course, this was not the prime time frequency. This was the same frequency that would support a community affairs program at 2 am.

This was the same frequency, time, and place that engendered the words Affirmative Action, Equal Opportunity, Diversity, Multiculturalism, Hispanic. These terms comfortably navigated the American Imagination. These words legislated a guilt-free Imagination that could embrace these terms but still argue that Art and Politics were separate.

The MFA allowed me to graduate into the study and shaping of the manifestations of these intellectual issues. The degree and my background allowed me in to the widest array of institutions that Houston had to offer, a deep slice of the American Imagination.

I could attend a wine party for a visiting writer who had just read at the Museum of Fine Arts, which would inform my writing class at The Chicano Family Center, which would inform the adjunct classes I taught at the University of Houston. I could argue about literary theory in the graduate student lounge, and then put into practice my beliefs about Art and Politics by designing a community writing class sponsored by Arte Público Press at Talento Bilingue de Houston.

And I began to experience more deeply just how Culture and Art shape each other.

Just as there are the words that lead up to a novel, there are words that lead up to the policies that lead up to the university that created an English Department and then a Creative Writing Program. There are rules and regulations that shape buildings out of the tumult that is a city.

We can be guided and blossom by the visions that inspire us, or we can be limited by the small, mean figures forged by legislation, demographics, and marketing as they exist. We do, after all, walk the paths laid by our visions.

During my apprenticeship, I continued to follow the work of Omar Casteñeda as he discussed the politics of aesthetics and also unleashed art that dramatized the red-hot edge of Politics and Art.

In 1997, I found out about his death, the news conveyed to me from the cover of his last published book—the story collection *Naranjo the Muse.*

In 1998, writer and activist Ishmael Reed chose my novel *The Aztec Love God* as the Winner of the Nilon Award for Excellence in Minority Fiction.

Casteñeda engendered "The Unspeakable/*Lo Que No Se Puede Decir*," the project in your hands. I inherited his vision for Latino Heretics. The excerpts included are from the novel *Islas Coloradas* which he completed just before his death.

"It is important to throw rocks at all institutions, but unlike some intellectual game-players, I seriously value the need humans have for institutions. The trick is to grow in one's

repertoire of institutions, to have the ability to function within them and to gain meaning from them, personal and social, and yet be able to leap into another at any given moment."
—Omar Castañeda in an interview for the *Americas Review.*

Instead of articulating my thoughts on Castañeda's thoughts, I would rather articulate some art inspired by the same muses that assaulted him.

These works should upset and disturb the gentlemen's agreements upon which some of the current politics of Latino identity are precariously based on, and also push writers to a new level of craft, a high style of writing—to upset the current politics of aesthetics as well.

This anthology goes beyond the popular magazine story of the moment: "Hispanic or Latino: Which Term is Better?" These works are highly crafted, yet they also rise above the muscle-show of aesthetics of writing that is just style that only squirms on the page and does not lead to action. These writers with hyper-art and hyper-heart can be as didactic as they wanna be.

And the revolution begins even before the first words are fired. The blend of writers undermines the protocol for anthologies. This collection unites writers not only from different parts of the country but also from different areas of writing and thinking.

Script writer, filmmaker, poet, short story writer, novelist, MFA-product, School-of-Hard-Knocks-Product, all Heretics, and each angry protester dictates the topics, but every entry aspires to the High Style—new thoughts, new forms, killer-prose that sabotages the politics of the English language, the politics of the Spanglish language. This art unites the best of several possible worlds under a Latino canopy and paves the way for a multi-multi-culturalism—an exponential-culturalism.

The old way, I would be pressed to define the "Heretic." This book, from the first page to the last page, is my first word in the definition.

These Heretics are not fighting at the surface level of which set of letters to call ourselves, but are creating art that is affected by the act of calling, are treading how this muscle in The

Tony Diaz

Imagination flexes to create these words, and how we use these words and how sometimes these words use us.

"They make a certain peace, with words a small portal to some place more meaningful than language. Between them, is not a word, but a meaningful lower growl and sibilant that is a shiver for them both. A shared and mutual shiver."
—From *Islas Coloradas* by Omar Castañeda.

Omar Castañeda

Omar Castañeda won the Fiction Collective Two's 1993 Nilon Award for Excellence in Minority Fiction for *Remembering to Say 'Mouth' or 'Face'*. His other works include the novel *Cunuman*, the young adult novels *Among the Volcanoes* and *Imagining Isabel*, a children's play, *Dance of the Conquest*, a picture book for children, *Abuela's Weave/El Tapiz de Abuela*, an edited collection of stories *New Visions: Fiction by Florida Writers*, and a collection of short stories *Naranjo the Muse*. *Islas Coloradas*, excerpted in this anthology, was his last novel.

Chapter 18 - Excerpt from *Islas Coloradas*

At first Gary listens with fascination at this strange and solitary voice in the woods. It draws him in, making him forget that he is lost in Totonepul, shins devoured by ants, lips cracked from thirst.

"You're in luck, you're in luck," the man screams. "Oh, yes, you're a lucky one to be sure, my friend. Came just at the right time for one of my best stews."

Gary is amazed that a human being can talk so much for so long with so little care as to whether he's being listened to or not. That alone sustains him as an audience—for a time.

" . . . Don't make it often and it's the rarity of the thing, partly, that makes it so special. Rarity often does that. It can even turn something normally thought of as awful or as beneath notice into something special—haute cuisine or, for that matter, haute culture. So, yes indeed . . ."

In the beginning, Gary tries to respond at every space that in normal conversation would require a nod, a "yes," an "I see," an "oh," or an "ah-huh," but it becomes all too apparent that no such thing is required, needed or, perhaps, even desired.

" . . .You came at a very good time. Not often I can catch monkey. Snakes, yes. They're easy enough so that the snake stew is not as rare as the snake and monkey stew. Monkeys are as hard to catch as humans. A little headhunter's joke. Yep, monkey and snake flavors blend. Some might oppose the juxtaposition, or shall we say the melding, of these two rather distinct flavors, but I believe they work extremely well together. You know, of course, the famous meal in Canton—now Guang Zhou—of The Battle Between The Tiger And The Dragon: civet cat and snake, usually python. You know the famous snake restaurant, with the glass window where you can pick your snake? Of course you do. Great mud-puppies there. Surely, you've been there. Had the bile in your maotai with a lady? Come on, wink wink, for that special energy, for that later course. Know what I mean, wink, wink— Monty Python, lad. Right, of course you have! Well this is modeled on that dish. The meal, I'm referring to, not the woman. I call it The Edenic Battle—with me as the winner."

Frank Carnegie throws back his head and laughs uproariously at his own joke. His laugh is deep, rich, coming from low in his belly. Gary is full of wonder at this man who not only talks incessantly, but who talks at the top of his lungs. He is thin from living in the woods, bedraggled, a hoary brown head, with twigs and leaf scraps caught in the tangles. He looks crazy as he seems.

It is impossible to carry on a real conversation. But Gary has already guessed that if he waits long enough, the man will come around to telling him what he wants to know and if not, well then, Gary can sometimes direct the deluge of words with shouted interjections that seep through the verbiage and queue up in the man's torrential consciousness for their turn to be refrained, reformulated, or assimilated, then spouted out from the central bureaucracy of his mind as if he himself had thought up the point.

"You see, the monkey represents man, and the snake, well, the snake represents The Snake. It is like a mixture of "This is not a Pipe,"—the famous painting which Max Ernst, Breton, Foucault and others discussed *ad nauseum*, and, of course, an emblematic 'problem' for language-prioritized theories—anyway, a mixture of that plus an intertextuality with Darwinian allusions working in the main. However, the monkey as signifier for man does indeed go back a great many centuries across cultures so that one can fairly say that that referent is prototypical—perhaps archetypal, not necessarily in the Jungian sense, however. I'm not much for Jungian approaches." He throws up his hands as if Gary were actually conversing with him, setting up a counter argument. "No, don't even talk to me about it. I've heard all the arguments—mostly by post-hippies and neohippies. It is all too hocus-pocus for me. Besides, the man wrote in the most awful prose. Completely contradictory and emotional. That was the style, however. You never really had to prove anything in the way we prove things today with statistics, careful logic and clearly precedented statements. Back then, one simply said things with a strong measure of authority and others bought the idea or not. The way things are done in English departments today, you know, or like French feminist critics. Like this article I once read in *Poets & Writers* about lambs being linked to the human heartbeat and fundamental to language. Language! Obviously a one-language speaker said that, if there ever was one. The writer meant it in the big sense: all languages. Of course, no linguist would ever say such a crazy thing, only someone who knows absolutely nothing about language. If the idea fits certain concerns in a field, then the idea is purchased, wholesale, as is, no questions asked, no return policy, caveat emptor. It strikes me that academia was far more overtly political then than now—perhaps not—which is not to say that academia of today isn't political, it's just that it is less overt—perhaps not.

"Reason number one hundred and ten why I left: You see, academia has been suffering from a great spiraling-down. But I wrote about this—Carnegie, 1980, that's the scholarly version; and *New York Times Review of Books,* on some little thing written by a goofball named Bloom. I love that word: goofball. That was the general consumption piece, in the *NYT.* No subtleties.

"You may have heard of me—no, that's right, you said you hadn't—well you didn't say it, you shook your head. Eat, son, eat."

Gary can only shake his head. It doesn't even matter, it seems, whether the man understands it as an insult or not.

"Shaking of the head is an interesting aspect of communication. Not every country makes the same gesture, you know. Gestures are quite fascinating. Yes, I wrote a very nice article—"Me, Iconicity and Pragmatics: This is Just to Say"—that contained a nice footnote on cultural variations of primal gestures like those used, for instance, to signify 'me.' Well, for some reason that caught the attention of many people. China was in the news and there was the bit about Chinese pointing at their noses to say 'me.' Also, I suppose being as simple as it was, it was the one thing my fellow academes could understand. Sorry lot, them. Pathetic state. English Departments, History Departments . . . they all lack depths— get it? Even Linguistics. Confused methodologies.

"I don't suppose Typology has made any more headway than when I left."

He does not register any response, but his own predisposed opinion. "No? Well, I'm not surprised with the generative obsession. That, no doubt, contributed to the general milieu for single-language study and the sophomoric extrapolation of the poet above-mentioned. Are you following me, boy? But I think it's also linked to the general practical attitude prevalent in linguistics and most studies—even related to things like the pseudo-science of Narratology. I mean, the fundamental approach is wrong-headed. Granted, it finally offers models that are utile— at least the Artificial Intelligence people know that: They don't care if the models are true to life, just so long as they are sufficient to create the illusion of life. Generative Linguists and Philosophers of Language, on the other hand . . . But don't get me started. Language Typology and Historical Linguistics. That's enough to say. That's the way of the future. No other way about it. You can't begin to understand Language until all languages and their proper evolutions are studied in a coherent systematic fashion. Let's hope linguists figure it out in time. Every day, data are lost on the evolution of languages. Yep: Hawkins, Thompson, Jepson, Li, these are people on the right track. Are they still alive? Hm? Oh. What is it you do again? And again and again?" He laughs at his own humor.

"Litera—" Gary tries to interject.

"Not a bad little joke. A sense of humor is very impor . . ."

"Literature!" Gary shouts.

". . . tant. Yes, that's right, literature. Well now, I seem to recall a little bit about that. Perhaps you've heard of me. No?

Well, I've written more than a little in that area, as well. Some called me the Midwestern U. S. Roman Jakobson. Only I spoke seventeen languages in American. You get it, right? My word, son, what is it you read, anyway? Let me explain the joke ... oh, never mind. You'd have to know much more than you do, much more, evidently. So eat, will you? I've had this monkey on my back forever. Eat."

Frank Carnegie talks even as he lifts a wooden spoon to his mouth. He holds the spoon directly in front of his mouth as he finishes speaking and then quickly inserts the stew.

"What brought you—" Gary tries to insert quickly, hoping against experience that there is some possibility of dialogue.

But Frank is already talking, miraculously speaking as he chews, or he holds the food to one side of his mouth while he speaks for several minutes. The food is like a wad of tobacco against his gums. "There is a definite change in attitude in studies. Gone is the desire to learn everything possible, to learn it well and to learn it for its own sake. Too much to learn about everything for the practical mind now. Too difficult and inefficient ..."

"... to be in Islas Coloradas?"

"... but I really think that one must try. Herculean task ... What? But that drive-learning, curiosity—is as basic as sex—Well, that's a long story, a long story to be sure, my coming here ..."

"Of course!" Gary says.

"... that bears repeating, to be sure. Ha-hah, get it? To be sure. Yes, well, I was a writer. No longer. I went away from linguistics and a brief interlude with socio-medical science—that was a very important time in my life. Well, but, I wrote fiction. Short fiction mostly. Maybe you've heard of me. Frank Carnegie. Hey, that rhymes, doesn't ..."

"You're the famous Frank Carnegie?" Gary is genuinely impressed, and not a little incredulous. It seems too impossible to even consider. It seems impossible that this non-stop lunatic could be the famous author of *Bitch and Biff Go Downtown to Meet the Dog-Face Girls, What We Mean, Meaning What We*

Do, and its sequel *Mean or Not Mean,* none of which Gary has read, though he has taught two of the books in introductory literature courses.

"... it. Sent my work along to all the usual places, you know. *Ohio Review, Georgia Review, Indiana Review,* all the state reviews, *Prairie Schooner,* etcetera, you know the ones. AWP clique. Associated Writing Programs. Have you ever heard of them? Yes, of course, you have. The neo-fascists of literature."

"Please ..."

"The story is one of woe, one of ..."

"... continue."

"... sadness and tribulation ..."

Gary rolls his eyes in self-mockery because, of course, Frank will continue. What on earth can stop this narration now? Anyway, Gary is now more interested, even though he feels the weariness of a reader with dense material.

"... that bears repeating."

"It begins in the summer of '62. Just kidding. In the chaos that is the random and undisciplined, yet catenated, set of characters that is one solitary person, in this case, yours truly. Long ago, you see, I was like a continent. I had islands and lakes and mountains and dozens of people inside me. I had native cultures and languages and transplanted peoples inhabiting the hills and vales, fishing along streams. Colonizing forces within, and insurgencies. I'm talking about me, you understand: me as made up of many people and issues—my, you're slow. These last had come to consider themselves native because it was their great-great grandparents who had first emigrated. I was a continent, you see. I was many things, internally. I had political strife. I had social upheaval. I had civil war. Not to mention the simultaneous foreign policies I had to constantly revise and adapt, not infrequently to the dismay of the citizenry, either. In all of this, I was mere *mesne lord*, if you will. But foreign policy is what this story is really about. Someone asked me how I got here and that, for now, will be a history of dealings with the world outside, not of domestic events. Foreign Policy. Suffice it to say, on the domestic side, a referendum was passed, a bill written and a policy enacted by a landslide vote. It was a public mandate.

"Again now, I, as foreign diplomat, was schooled in Chicago. You may have heard of the University of Chicago. It has some reputation. I received my degree in linguistics, with courses in anthropology. But that's not important. Or is it? Let's see. No, not now. Right reserved, however, to back-track."

"Why the hell not," Gary throws out as if he is talking to the tree beside him. He wonders how much more he can take.

"Where was I? Linguistics at the University of Chicago—cozy place, like a monastery. If it weren't for Jimmy's, I tell you, the mind of many a young ectomorph would have snapped. No sports . . ."

"Writing!" Gary yells.

" . . . no attention to the body. A highlight of the year is the Latke-Hamentash Symposium. Scholars from all disciplines come with their papers, having written them—Writing?—in all seriousness, to deliver for this multimedia event that debates relative virtues between the round potato pancakes and the triangular ones. Writing?

"Yes, writing in linguistics was fun and serious, but, as I said, the field was not ready for typology and historical linguistics—and I don't mean philology, either! It wanted generativists, semanticians, syntacticians—and not diachronic syntax—and those pseudo-linguists, applied linguists, teachers of English as a second language. Poor Chomsky . . . so coopted in his language work, so abandoned in his true work. Don't get me started. Or speech pathologists. . . ."

"Hey!" Gary says, but let's it go when he sees that it isn't going to register.

" . . . Those few positions of theoretical linguistics had firmly entrenched scholars. They made hay while they could. So, I began to write articles in popular science magazines, like Carl Sagan—maybe you've heard of him. That writing took me to fiction, after all I was already fictionalizing by creating maps that were ever simpler, ever reductionist in their representation. That's what fiction is, in part. A seductive reduction. Even the most complex works are alluring representations that necessarily simplify. The illusion of complexity is there, but it is merely a skeleton. The clever arrangement of bones tricks the reader into layering on flesh from the many maps of his or her experience of life. A work of literature is the interstice between authorial skeletons and a reader's total collection of maps of the world, those self-made and those handed down. But that's another topic. Think about it later.

"So, I wrote volumes. Stories, poems, novels, collections. I sent them out and they came back with rejection after rejection. I watched my ideas and my contrivances dismissed by editors who themselves wrote nonsense. I looked around and saw journal after journal filled to overflowing with what can only be called masturbatory realism. Writers, somewhere, somehow, had fallen in love with literature of identification. At the same time writers repudiated the traditional views of the specialness of literature and the traditional notions of moral fiction—á la Gardner—they unwittingly became ultrareactionaries: Underlying their work was the notion that fiction owed some allegiance to reality, that it ought to be chaotic because life is chaotic, that fiction ought to be strange, subjective, immediate, because life is such an amalgam of all disciplines, that the contemporary world has access to everything all at once, that immediacy, subjectivity, and the juxtaposition of widely disparate elements is apart of our world. This, no doubt, is when the first-person, present-tense syndrome began. Post-modernism, you see. Zero writing. We need not enter the equations of Vico, Saussure, Pierce, Barthe, *ad scholarae contemporanum*. Though I do admire Eco, and the writer Calvino, and that fellow Culler."

Actually, Gary likes them too. They are inventors of new worlds. They don't go on in first-person alone, just as Carnegie said. It is true, that like poetry, first-person narrations are the most difficult to achieve their fullest potential, while being the easiest to do badly. That's why beginning writers go to poetry and first-person.

"But what matters, my *rheme*, is that the literary journals were infected with a reactionary view of literature while purporting to be avant-garde. It is reminiscent of those young people who spike their hair, paint it all manner of bright colors to scoff at the traditional while having the politics of Richard Nixon and the morality of Billy Graham. You can't find more conservative people as those who are the most outrageous on the surface. Literature is no different, my friend. Literary magazines are full of high-gloss surfaces built upon aesthetics that harken to previous centuries. Fiction owes allegiance to its own conventions, not to life. Fiction owes allegiance to a driving outward, to experiment, at the same time that it owes its allegiance to its own history. There is a gentle discord, an elegant strife: forces that move away and forces that bind. Literature has its own paradox of langue and parole, the weak and strong forces, pal o' mine. Don't forget, you heard it here first. The physics of literature. Literature's weak force is that which urges the artist outward into uncharted realms—radiation, if you will; the strong force is that which mandates a dependency on conventions, on intertextuality, on expectations. Binding the nucleus. Bodies fall apart, or collapse, with an inchoate balance of these forces. Swinging to one extreme or the other is swinging to one demise or another. At any given time, a work of worth, like a stable atom, must be dominated by the strong force: It is the allegiance to its own conventions, its own history, its traditions, its nuclear cohesion. Yet no structure, except perhaps those impenetrable Black Holes, is without its combative weak forces, as well. We all want to write a work of sufficient energy to unify all four forces!

"Well, you may imagine it as torque, or as a gorgeous complementarity of position and velocity. Difference *et Differance*, as Derrida liked to chew his cud on. Ah, it's been too long since I've thought of all this noon-sense, these sun-dry things.

What is it again? Weak force is leopards and hadrons? Strong force is neutron, proton binding or deuteron state—Crap! I'm out of practice, my little gluon. My Latin's rough. Maybe the electromagnetic force and gravity would be a better analogy, or electromagnetic and strong. This is all too long ago! Anyway, these things matter, even if they ain't-i-matter here."

Frank Carnegie sputters in laughter, spewing out pieces of stew, before continuing. Gary wipes his legs.

"Because what matters . . . yes, yes, what matters we discuss, eh? What matters is that literary journals became dominated by this reactionary avant-garde. Parrot writers! The great gyring-down, I call it. The proliferation of M.F.A. writers and programs. The plutocracy of the AWP: wealth measured in publications, particularly publications in journals edited by members of the AWP. But that is the great aristocratic way, to define the measure of wealth cleverly enough—from the very start—to eliminate all others who would be able to compete. Set up rules that only you know! That's the key, my potato skin. The great gyring down: Those accepted into the programs were those most likely to produce material like that published in the programs' journals; those publishing wore the appropriately spiked hair; those who became teachers had proven their willingness and ability to parrot. Krawk! And just as the great gyring down occurred in Education Departments all over the country so that one day we woke up and saw the shambles around us. I woke up and saw the literary ruins. Let me tell you there was little love left. There was not sufficient depth for love to exist, so love beached itself and its lungs collapsed under its own weight. A whale of an end! I saw the writing on the books. I saw the genre-ization of literary works."

Despite himself, Gary wonders if this was when the man stopped using "he said/she said's" in his fiction. That trick, another irony of diminished artifice. He thinks that he wouldn't mind hearing what the famous Frank Carnegie has to say about that. But the torrent of words soon kills that desire.

"I had one editor read a story and say that a line in it was too jarring, that it was out of tone, voice, character, completely out of order because it was sexist. The line could be interpreted as being sexist only if the line was read completely out of tone, out of character, and out of voice. Yet instead of seeing that he ought to read the line in tone, in voice, and in character to discover what it might mean, he decides that the line has to go. You don't understand, do you? You see, virtually every utterance can be understood in a variety of ways, the most correct way being that which fits in the context, of course. Context is composed, naturally, of voice, tone, character, etcetera. You following this? There are some fifty-six ways of understanding the word 'no,' depending on hand gestures, intonation, character, environment, what went before it, what went after. Do you see? Try this sometime: say 'no' while placing one hand at various points on your head—over mouth, one eye, side of head, front of head, things like that—and your other hand either on your hip or at your side and see how each 'no' changes meaning just by placement of the hands. In fact, I've always wanted to write a long work where everything was conveyed through gestures. No dialogue, just descriptions of stance, gesture, facial expressions. What a work that would be: the non-verbal in a basically verbal form! *This is not a work of language!* it would say. Of course, it would be a very culture-specific work, but perhaps no more than usual. And doomed. It would be like writing in a hyperbolic style today: No one understands it; they think it's outmoded baroque rather than humor. Maximalism out, minimalism still in vestige. People can't read any more.

"Anyway, rather than interpreting from these contextual aspects, the editor came to my line—no doubt from the side—and forced one interpretation. Once that was done, the editor would not back down. He was blind to all other possibilities. You understand? Yes? No?

"To be fair, though, I am not a great writer. Maybe barely above good. You see," he says, crouching with a stick in hand to draw a graph, "There is a kind of Bell Curve in this regard.

On the vertical axis we can plot success as measured by publications, thusly."

He draws his complete chart in a patch of sandy ground:

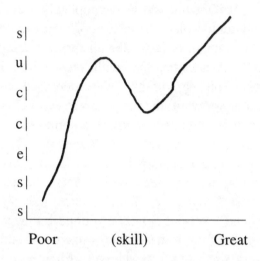

s |
u |
c |
c |
e |
s |
s |

Poor　　　　(skill)　　　　Great

"Along the 'y' axis is the skill level of the writer. One can see that—and there has been research on exactly this aspect (e.g. Carnegie, 1980)—that there is a sharp decline in success just after mediocrity and then another sharp increase after what may be termed the good skill level and once into the great skill level. I have to admit that I was in this middle range: neither mediocre nor great. Simply good. Until, that is, my final straws, where I became mediocre and famous."

And crazy as an asparagus farm, Gary thinks. Stark, raving lunatic!

"There were two last straws, my bosom-pal. I received a rejection for a story and scrawled at the bottom of the form was the comment, 'Not in first-person.' The other was a book jacket that praised the book because it had immediacy even though written in the third-person. I quickly surveyed the literary journals. I randomly selected one thousand magazines and six journals and discovered that eighty-six percent of the fiction was in first-person point of view. Fifty-eight percent was present-tense. Every single story had overt explication. Every single story told you exactly what it was doing. Gone the subtle fitting together by the reader; gone reading as combination and divination. Left was surface mapping.

"Of course, I immediately set up my computer with global search and replace lists: 'was' to 'is'; 'had' to 'has'; 'did' to 'does.' I devised a program, in C+, to determine '-ed' endings that should be '-es' and those that should be '-s' endings. I searched and replaced and then worked my spell-checker and changed every single story into a present-tense, first-person narration. I dumped all the stories that had a certain affinity between form and content and changed everything into linear narrations. I avoided all echoes within. Images and metaphors were used only if they did not relate to one another. I took out ninety-five percent of the commas and contractions.

"I got published. Not a little, either. I never sent a story out more than three times before an editor took it. Maybe you've heard of me. Finally, my fame arrived when I wrote my novel, *The Liver King,* with each chapter alternating between first, third and second person, and between past and present tense. I wiped out any possibility of significance to these shifts. Characters repeated in the chapters, but nothing happened that connected between them, and I did nothing that related to the title until the final chapter when one of my characters became Liver King of the Fahquene Slaughter House Festival. The book was a monstrous success. It was marvelous. I deliberately told stories from the point of view of children and filled the pages with exact names of flowers, animals, trees, things no child—nor any adult layperson!—could every know. Only a botanist would know the names of so many flowers and trees. Either that or a writer who went to a book and looked the stuff up. Editors said I was the most descriptive writer they had read. Editors said I had mastery over voice and character. I deleted all contractions and wrote in the second-person. I had first-person narrators die in present-tense! My stories were swallowed up, ripped from pages and stuffed into maws that cawed and burped for more tripe—you don't laugh, do you?"

Gary gives a forced chuckle.

"Well, I got a little fame. Perhaps you've heard of me: Frank Carnegie. I was offered academic jobs. I was offered guest editorships. I was awarded grants. I had fellowships named after me. I did, as they say, Okay."

"So what—?"

"There are those who would wrongly think it was failure that sent me flying from my country. It was success. Younger writers began copying my style and winning awards and getting academic positions and teaching even younger writers how to write in the same way. But it wasn't until the sixtieth anniversary of the Iowa Workshop, that I saw the arrogance of present-tense. It was there that I finally saw the brazen nature of standing outside of time. Present-tense is hubris. Present tense, first-person is hubris of the highest order. At the anniversary, we all watched an angry man point out the Emperor's naked butt; I watched the clamoring congregation pull the hapless man down. He accused them of being untutored in the traditions of their art, of not having read outside the ultimately parochial realm of their country. He may have called them White or Pasty-faces, I don't remember. He implied the parrot syndrome that I had seen and had already sold-out to. The crowd went wild, of course. The man was throwing pies at their sacred icons. Needless to say—terrible phrase that—they grappled the man off the stage and choked him with balls of purple and orange hair that were ripped from the idolaters' heads. They beat him about the head and shoulders with rolled up *AWP Chronicles*, crushing his ribs and blackening his cheeks with ink. I believe the poor man expired under the tonnage of invisible clothes."

"As for me, I backed away, guarding my front all the time. I moved back from that frothing crowd and into the street. I backed up to my car, parked at the very head of the lot, nearest the podium. I backed into my car and drove in reverse all the way to the airport where a flight to Islas Coloradas was just reviving its engines.

Omar Castañeda

"The huge rotors coughed, farted, then caught as they set up a roar of wind and dust and debris, and tinged with the faintest hint of something that excited all those waiting to board, infecting them with a delicious tension that they interpreted as promise, or hope, or an auguring of good fortune. And I, too, became swept up in the goodbyes and the breathiness—I knew within myself that I had to forever leave my present tense and re-acquaint myself with something slower, something more honest with the continuity of human expression. The present-tense had stolen all continuity from me. I had to get it back. Islas Coloradas promised regeneration, some hope. Seriously.

"Here's my advice: Read with an open mind, don't sweat the small stuff, and let things percolate. Never, ever, reduce anything to a single paragraph or sentence. You'd be surprised what things live on in the memory, what images linger and how the mind ties it all together."

Gary imagines tying him up, gagging him, perhaps.

"Be that as it may, I lived awhile in Santa Luz, working the terraces, then into the shoals with fishermen, then into the lumber mills of Petén, then into these jungles to find the legendary women of Ligalgan. Here in these woods, I cry out, I speak out. I glory in speech. It is my task in life to bring the news to the world, to sketch out truths so the very gods will see we are not slouching toward Gomorrah, but are yet crawling from its gates. Language holds the key, my relative clause. Language is the marvel and the blessing. Language is the map of our minds and of our hearts. Language is the tunnel in, it—but it is a mistake to think like Sapir-Whorf, you know.

"This is a mistake that so many naifs make. This idea that language constrains what we can know or that it defines our world. Stupid idea. Only someone with no real understanding of the world's languages and the world's diversity of expression could believe that to such an extent as freshman composition teachers believe it. A language can express anything it wants to express. When a need arises, a language can meet that need. Otherwise it

29

is no language at all. Productivity distinguishes a true language from if artificial language. As does flex and the dynamic tension between *langue* and *parole*—so like strong and weak forces, tradition and deviation, archetypes and incidentals, genotypes and phenotypes, maps! Cartography! The principle of the mutually exclusive residing in one body! Complementarity! Kafka knew this well. His humor lies in reveling in it: 'Nein, in Wirklichkeit; im Gleichnis hast du verloren.'

"Let me tell you, friend o'mine, language . . ."

Tony Diaz

"Take Me" From *Sombrero Hysteria*

At the age of twenty, youths who wanted to become warriors went to war. But first the youth's parents approached the veteran warriors with food, drink, and gifts, to seek a sponsor to take their son to war. They took great care of the youths in wars, and they showed the youths how to take captives once the tide turned in the Aztecs' favor.

From Aztec Warfare *by Ron Hassig*

You feel everyone in the *zocalo* ignoring him, casting their glances away from the place he occupies, as if there was a point overlooked in the creation of this sun, and that hole is right where he is standing, inside *your* market, among the arrows, the pots, the statues that *your* emperor, that *your* merchants have summoned or delivered, that *you* helped guard.

And this extreme is as embarrassing as giving him more attention than he deserves, but there he is, dragging by a thick chord a stack of high white cotton cloths that gleam next to his dark red-brown skin. Even then, you can tell that he is not really dragging the cotton. It is part of his resistance to be barely pulling it, as if he were not a captive, as if he were still a part of The Empire, and not an ex-warrior, as if he could still kill you even though his hair is past the length for a warrior.

The fat scab-scars straight across his forehead, just above his brow, mean he showed promise as one of The Empire's best potential killers, best grabber of sacrifices, best plunderer of subjects and families, a true Aztec. That head is filled with pictures from inside the Mexica empire, inside that golden door. They taught him what is to be taught residents of an empire, behind their walls of water, behind their large army, above the temple stairs, Aztecs.

And even if he did not have the chance to kill or capture the way he could, he has at the very least stood closer than you to the killers-of-many.

But now he is a prisoner of *your* state. Alive, deprived of the honor of death in battle or on an altar. And you wonder how that could be, how powerful, how skillful one of *your* own soldiers, the defenders of *your* empire, someone that *you* might have been born next to, how could someone like *you* have mustered the strength to stun, almost kill the Aztec enough to pull him from his purpose in life because fighting, you believe, must be the only thing that makes their hearts beat.

And he is not only darker than you. He is almost a different shade of red-brown, as if he is privileged to a part of the sun that will never shine on you.

And those Cactus Eaters do many different things to themselves so that you can notice one of them whether a captive or prince in a crowd.

They have mastered the accumulation of covert then overt signs that build up to an Aztec and then an Aztec Empire that leads them to kill after soldiers have surrendered, to rape the women of the towns they occupy, to kill the children who might some day grow to be fine killers-of-Aztecs.

And those lines across his head are flashes and signs that shout: I am a Cactus Eater. I will rape your wife. I will kill your brother.

You grab at the shiny white layers of cotton and pull. "Stand still, Cactus Eater."

His long hair moves with your jerk.

He expertly turns and hits you with his obsidian eyes.

Don't call the arrow war an arrow war. Call it "war when the corn grows."

Don't call the Flower War a Flower War. It is actually "war when the corn is picked."

* * *

Don't believe that you become a god when you die in battle. Someone else will simply be given your stones to carry for the next emperor's tomb.

Don't call me a slave. I am free of military service. I am free of land. I am free of family. I am free of tribute. I am free of honor. I know that to be unceremoniously murdered right here, right now or to be ceremoniously murdered on the sun pyramid— I know that these are the same deaths. And because of this, I am the emperor of the slaves free of empires. And my role in painstakingly sustaining the perfect environment for the emperor's erection is limited. And you, you are the balls of society.

My vengeance for the death of Tizoc, who I now know as the Emperor of Peace, began before I was aware. And the vengeance that has not been met even after Tizoc's name was changed by history is my vengeance for the murder of the splendor of the empire, the killing of the Mexica's true spirit, my vengeance for the murder of the power, the beauty, the wisdom of the children of the sun.

As Tizoc's murder was being planned, perhaps even being carried out, the priests unleashed the visions of the Invisible Plague, the Invisible Famine through songs, through the naming of children, through the re-naming of days, through the reported whispers of gods, through the way the priests stare as they walk, in the fact that the priests bothered to walk among the roads of the commoners.

The signs that the priests were inspiring in the Mexica affected my hearing, shaped my cultivated rage in such a way that I could hear the corn growing.

When I would rest from my military training I would sit, concentrate, let the fatigue of my body evaporate in the air and I could hear my father, The Corn Merchant, getting fatter, his skin ripping to grow with his insides as his abundance increased;

all that corn. And even for me, it was difficult to accept that there were so many people to pick the corn instead of it and them being used to create war to raise the sun and the princes in battle.

And the priests' signs and my rage had shaped my sight as well.

As I trained and rested and trained and listened and waited for a noble to select me as his student for The Flower War that did not arrive for the nobles who were becoming more hostile towards us, I began to experience visions.

As the empire's aura starved, I dreamed of the Jaguar Knights as walking skeletons, the jaguar skin on their backs sagging, the hollowed head of those beasts wobbling on their shrunken heads, fasting without the thick black hair on their heads to hold them in place, the meat from their skulls gone. I saw the quetzal feathers dyed blue, red, green and gold, orange, placed, I saw that they were placed carefully along where the full arch of a strong back should command strength, barely making the bulk they were ordered to create. Cocked plumes, bent feathers. I saw one, then many, then a race of the walking dead.

During the day, when the sun managed to raise its feeble head, short days, as we trained in our martial arts, the nobles would attend our exercises in their full regalia to show us what we did not have, what we could not have without a fight.

But I interpreted my dreams to mean that I could defeat the walking dead who did not carry sunlight. I knew I was stronger, had deeper vision, and could handle more heat from the sun, that burning on my skin during sparring, during my training, I knew the burning on my skin comes from the inside and burns brighter in me in battle.

They were short-tempered.

Jade Fist, captor of Mountain-Warrior, who captured Twenty-Hands, who captured Star Fighter, all of whom whose total sacrifices added up to 110 good works—Jade Fist had even struck a jar merchant's son dead during a sparring match as if to demonstrate what a noble could do in peace if there was not war to satisfy the gods he had satisfied and was forced to satisfy.

I would see them in this mock splendor and from behind they were still the skeletons of my sleep.

From the back, the Eagle Knights' wooden helmets, shaped like the eagle's mouth by subjugated artisans, rattled hollow. Regalia floated on the frames of men as if those men were ready to disappear. The cotton armor, the feathered capes, the decorated helmets all floated.

But then I would look them in the face. And they were men again. For a brief moment.

You will be happy to know that the Aztecs *will* fall. The Aztecs will be slaves. The Aztecs will all be murdered.

And this began occurring before the Mexica nobles protested that Tizoc was scared of war, that Tizoc cowered in peace and that this peace was wasting their precious youth and preventing the kingdom from advancing through their advancement.

It was not Tizoc nor Peace that will kill the Aztecs. It is the hardening of bloodlust in the way the corn is grown, in the fact we have a War Season just as we have a harvesting season, it is the fact that it sounds as if it is the same thing to say "a cactus grows in the sun" as it is to say "a pyramid grows with war."

There was less war, and we were accustomed to a certain number of deaths, mourning, grief. It was odd for the sun not to shine on our anguish. And though there were fewer deaths, from the war, fewer of our own captured, there still were some losses.

Young warriors of the ripening age would disappear in the night, would leave for their wealthy fathers' homes from the military schools and never arrive, or leave the house and try to get to our schools and never make it. They were taken up by the sun. They were victims of the invisible famine, they were consumed by the starving sun who could not sleep and would wander the earth looking for blood just to survive, but if this went on too long it would stop rising. It needed blood.

Once enough merchants', enough artisans' sons were consumed by the lurking, nocturnal sun, they began to ask the priests for the questions to ask to understand what was happening, and they were taught to ask why the sun was picking up children at night, and then taught to ask why the sun was angry, and then were taught to ask for more signs of the Invisible Famine.

Then there were more omens.

And then we were told Tizoc was murdered.

This I can see, awake, not asleep, not in a vision.

A ritual of treason. Where the Aztec advisors acting in our own good held open the door and bowed a welcome to the emissaries of the violence of the enemy who needs war too, and the Emperor's guards protected him by making sure he would not flee, and he had no choice but to drink from the chalice the harsh, hot result of his dreams, visions. To swallow his words in bitter poison. And his death would motivate the fire, perfectly inspire the fire of the violence he tried to extinguish.

I was picked by the Jaguar Knight—Obsidian Cactus, captor of Feel-No-Pain, who captured Sky Shield, who captured Bearer-of-Mother-of-All-Swords, through all of whom had passed the lives of 203 men of stature.

And this was a far better humiliation than I suspected my father's corn-wealth, my father's station in life, and my attitude could ever buy. For the nobles were eager to not accept my father's gifts to grant me the privilege of serving as their second, their apprentice, their servant in one of their Flower Wars. This was in part because there were simply not enough wars, so families were paying more and more, there was a bounty of fortunes for the honor of putting sons in danger. Another part of this was that there was simply something about me . . . something . . . in my attitude . . . something about me *they* did not like.

I enjoyed the women who prepared us warriors in the secret dens for the secret life, the women who showed us the bliss of the universe many, many times.

But *that* was the second bliss of the universe for me because the first bliss, the first bliss is this. . . .

I wanted the women, the wives that war brings. I wanted the mantles of honor, the quetzal feathers that make you glow, that give you the spirit of honor, that create a wall around you that parts people before you arrive, that moves people in a crowd, that make you a pressure that can be felt even if you are not seen. But this *alone* is not the first bliss of the universe.

When I had brought down my obsidian on an enemy during the Arrow Wars, when the arrows fall like an avalanche to kiss prince and commoner alike, when I killed my first man in battle, I felt that bit of sunlight that everyone has, returned to the sun. I could feel it run through me when it left them. And that bright shiny moment, *that* is the fist bliss of the universe.

The emperor feels this supremely, and handles it for the people. He is the closest to the sun, and how he directs this light shapes the empire.

True-priests and true-warriors understand this, but differently, and only parts.

And the nobles, the nobles are just fools who do not know anything about this. They only understand the effects, the manifestations, not the source. This talent, to ignore the source, and to focus on its crumbs, this talent makes you a good corn-merchant, a seller-of-gourds, an excellent politician.

A true-priest can detect someone who experiences the sun differently than the false-priests, false-warriors, and control him.

But there is a way to understand your experience of the sun but still participate in the nobles' world of manifestations but that requires rising above everything you have been taught, above the way spirit is expended into words. It requires ignoring the history of the pyramids, the whispered complaints of the stones splashed with drops of blood, the hum of the chalice, the desire of the jade not to be shaped, the gold's coquette smirk.

And this is what Tizoc must have been able to do.

He bore true-light. He possessed knowledge of the system enough to become emperor. But was separate enough from it to desire to wage and wait for just-wars. He wanted to shape the sunlight into peace. No one less than a subversive had come to rule the Empire.

His failure was that he desired to lead the world in a new direction from the tip of the pyramid, as if to be at the pinnacle was enough. But he did not know that even there he was still under the watchful eye, in our eyes, under The Sun—which was turned into the ultimate pinnacle in the event a Tizoc should not only exist but somehow get to rule.

Someone like this, the nobles with their trained glances can detect. And control. Eventually.

And that was why I was a gamble.

I have always been subversive. It is in my blood. My father conquered it in himself which made it easier for the empire to conquer that blood in him, and they rewarded him for that conquest. Society rules, and he learned, understood and accepted the rules of society. He learned the ways of corn in society, and society paid him for his knowledge and corn. With that gift he could afford to sacrifice my help during the harvest and allow me to train. My father's sacrifice for the Flower War was a gentle gamble to try and complete the harvest of his crops without his son who stalked the most stalks, tore the most cobs, leaf and all, who left stalks bent, leaves in the yellow, and they could always find my sacks of corn piled high in abundance with green bits from leaves and stalk, piled high, dented, slammed one on the other, bruised ripe corn.

There was always something in me that alluded the empire's grasp.

They could not break open my skull. And that was why I was a gamble. That was why nobles were not quick to take my father's wealth. I was not empire-blind. For me, the empire created the world that created the wars that opened the path for short moments into that brilliant frenzy where every movement, every act decides if I or you are to continue existing or not.

An Aztec Second, unlike other seconds or even other empire's firsts, in a Flower War not only carries the extra weapons, the extra shields, guards the extra horde of feathers, he also must carefully place them on the weapons as they are brought from battle by the third-seconds, exchanged for new weapons. The Aztec second has studied how to repair, polish, and renew the weapon with the vitality of the new feathers so that each stroke of the weapon conveys the power, the prestige, the unlimited resource, wealth, the unlimited power, the unlimited soldiers, the unlimited frenzy, the aura of the empire. And this must be done at a level of spirit just above the frenzy on the battle field of the Flower War. A second must posses the presence of mind that the fate of the Empire rests on the special and correct placement of each bit of obsidian, each feather placed on the club.

But my flaw, as an Imperial Corn Picker was that I truly enjoyed the frenzy. The emperor, the empire, this sun, and these gods were good for giving me the tools to enjoy this frenzy and to heighten it with victims, with the threat of the sweet nectar of no-life, they added the necessity to muster the right struggle to drag off someone from the world, someone who wanted to remove me or someone who at least dearly wanted to remain in the frenzy.

I was a gifted and talented killer, but The Empire needed me to learn how to control that frenzy as it moved through me, to know when to step just short of the kill when we were shown the point in the battle when the emperor, the priests, and the gods, demanded prisoners. I had been provided with as many possibilities for captives that an Arrow War can provide, but I destroyed these opportunities.

We must pull from war some men and kill them after the frenzy of the battle, in the calm of the passion of a ritual, and invite their emissaries, their leaders who think they are brave in attending this trap from which the princes want you to walk away from, changed, with a message for your people, a message that you will not need to repeat, which they will read on your face. So that they will shudder when our names are uttered, and at the thought of us in battle, so that when we do fight, we will conquer you even more easily, and take yet one more away from you, until the next battle.

* * *

After my third Arrow War, I was at the age of shame
for having taken no captives, but I had eliminated a dozen of
The Aztec's overt enemies. At the ceremony where captures
are verified, extolled, and rewarded, because I was not a cow-
ard, and because I had killed under the mantle of the empire, I
was not ruined with the signs of shame. I was allowed to shave
half my head, at least. And I was not ordered to wear the colors
of one who has run from battle in fear, or has been unsuccessful
in too many battles. I was simply a gifted and talented killer, but
the nobles wanted a catcher-of-sacrifices.

So the priests blessed me with their attention, and cut into
me the importance of sacrifices. Laid me down and tried to cut
into my head the importance of war for them.

On the altar of no-death, they rained on me the small cuts
on my head, with jade kisses that said, "Here moves the base
spirit of the Aztecs, with mind and movement even beyond our
own desire, control him, and you will find only the base."

And this settled the hum in my head, cultured me into the
finer aspects of decorum. And I did not want my head cut again.
This reformed by spirit. This measure of composure helped. As
did my father's promise of one year of corn-food, one year of
material transport, one stalk of quetzal feathers for the Jaguar or
Eagle Knight who would then accept my risk. This created the
ripple that would wiggle up the pyramid to the spot where a noble
felt the whim to bestow me. And then Tizoc was murdered.

And I knew I would stop—just right. I would wound to
almost dead, and drag back the near-corpse to be regally murdered—I swore. And I could taste the strong, dull—that taste of
blood in my mouth. And when I envisioned this most vividly, I
would realize I was biting my own tongue.

My war paint was simple, thick fibers from the maguey
my mother mixed in it. I smelled green, like the insides of the

maguey, and the paint was thick, not shiny on me, and I could feel the fibers from the maguey paint squirm on me.

My arm looked covered on mistake, not painted for war. And the wrong things stuck to me.

I caught dust, dirt. I felt flecks of the empire on my skin, and I smelled like a maguey, guts cut open, green. And the stench siphoned my rage. And I realized why I must wear it. The maguey paint, that I was ordered to use, that was in the noble book of the emperors' desire for war, that paint said everything about me to the princes around me so that I would not be mysterious to them. They have seen my kind before, they have killed my kind before, and I will work myself out, one way or the other. Everything they cared to know about me, anything that was important to them, was smeared all over me, and the smell, the early morning dew stink ate away at my rage. And I was aware of my skin, how it hardened in places, how it cracked, how the paint magnified. Since I was a First-Second I was required to carry my sword, but when it was handed to me, covered as I was, it was the first time in my life that it felt heavy.

We march barefoot, behind Obsidian Cactus, who wears the costume of the Eagle Warrior, black feathers and he is bright with white and gold trimming, and he looks twice as heavy with the cotton armor under him, the Eagle helmet.

We march two days, his First in front of us we seconds, in front of thirds, in front of the women, who we must also protect from distracting spirits.

And Obsidian Cactus does not say and does not need to say a word to us. We walk in a line of the well-trained and thoroughly indoctrinated, each place in line attributed to a greater plan for the march, no matter how long, to the Flower War: the weapons, the feathers, the obsidian bits, the food, the women, all of us barefoot for our place in this war which has a pattern in the stars we are told.

We walk to a field where a battle is waging, and has been waging, and perhaps is still waging, and the wide field of War

When the Corn is Picked is nothing like War When the Corn Grows. Here, there are only bright feathers, high helmets. It is pretty to watch the waves of feathers move back and forth, like an ocean of random feathers come alive moving like shooting stars. 100 nobles versus 100 nobles, who will come and go off the field but will always be 100.

There are signs to let us know how the war goes, but they are basic to Arrow Wars as well: Red smoke means "Petals shower the ground." Black smoke means "It is morning for the cactus." What this means will change during the course of the battle, from attack to attack, from leader to leader, and in this case, from Eagle Knight to Eagle Knight to his First, First-Seconds, and Third-Seconds, and servant women. But there it is ever more clear that in the smoke that my lot has been cast or ignored. I walk, trying to predict my prediction.

Then we must stand still, at each of the four directions and guard Obsidian Cactus, as he sits, legs crossed, and concentrates to attain the level of spirit of the Eagle. And the First applies the paint, as trained, that will ease our warrior into the tumult. He goes within. I cannot imagine it, but sense echoes of it that I interpret into frenzy but that He could contain.

I feel him breathe deeper, I can see the black and white feathers over his back raise, and get darker, to fill with the air of the flying-eagle, I can feel the cotton armor evaporate as he is lighter than air and strong in the lightness and swiftness. I understand and sense that his costume, body, and weapons must remain intact, as close to intact as they were the moment he reached the place where he is allowed to soar. And we must renew that moment as best that we can when we take him his next shield, sword, obsidian, and renew and imbue it with the spirit of that moment.

But than I am caught, in a flash, by a misfit spirit, a troubled god, that showed me in one second the moment I would receive my animal-skin battle uniform, and it would be made out of my family's skin, my father's skin, my own skin. I would

recognize my own mottled splotches, my age marks, my flesh
tear-stained from sadness and pulls.

We are only a small part of this ritual. We merely add to
its excitement because we add to the luck of the ritual, slightly
change the set variables that they are familiar with, reorganize
their pieces.

And the younger of us still believe we can aspire, we
can soar with the Eagles and Jaguars, and there are some who
have, so there are many who believe they are destined to be the
exception to the rule, and they are the unexpected, ungauged,
the exciting-to-watch fervor.

And that is the first moment I truly pray for the corn to
stop growing.

What War When The Corn is Picked is to me is the crushed
maguey behind the feathered backs of the Eagle Knights and the
Jaguar Knights. The Rose War is the back of their helmets as
they dance with their enemies, speak to each other in a body language, dance, transmit signals in dances. I cannot break down
into signs, into the messages they transmit to each other to catch
each other during the dance that dictates the upper echelon of my
society, which too I cannot break down into signs, which I can
only see from far away, from the crushed maguey.

I follow the First, who knew the path of our Eagle, the
First who can walk further into the invisible circles around the
battlefield, around our warrior, that we must respect. And he can
go further than I, but I must still watch him who must watch our
warrior to know when he needs to be renewed.

The ground we pass is covered with crushed feathers. But
you don't dare pick them up. Because it is filth now. No, it is
gold. Weapons lie in the dirt, feathers from Tlacala, but if you
touch it this way, if you did not capture or kill someone for it, you
are filth. And as valuable as they are is how much less valuable
you will be afterwards.

And there is blood on the floor, too.

War to me is a distant chant, a hum. It is a mysterious

noise that we men cannot make with others of our kind, our family, neighbors. It is the yells that we can make only when our yells join our enemy's noise as we shout for blood, for captives, as we bolster our bodies for fight, flight, fright, for blood, to fend off, to fend on.

War is the evaporating hum of the battle as I approach, the noise of it dissipating as I move toward it, the sound of glory flying away. I live in the rustle of its feathers, and there in front of me, like contaminated jewels littered on the floor, feathers I covet but cannot touch.

We cannot simply join the costume and color of the princes' fray; we common soldiers are fighting your princes and as well as ours. And the sun is just a bright orange prop.

It was then that I saw a hungry warrior interrupt the battle-dance of two nobles at the front of the War When the Corn is Picked.

And he was covered like me, in the maguey paint, but with chunks, thick drops of the paint, covering his skin like scales, where mine had cracked and sagged, his was like the snake skin, his head shorn on one side, covered in bright red paint dimmed by the maguey paint, but for him, he looked more ferocious, more vicious than the princes, than I even aspired or deluded myself to be.

I saw him walk through all the invisible circles that we are taught to respect, taught to avoid, told that we would complicate the Aztec world, the world of our leaders, introduce an alien element to the complex and brilliant battle plan of our rulers who had a sense of the field and every soldier there, who must know who is on the field, the sacred battle field, and their powers, and the invisible circle ebbs and flows, and the battle dictates its expanse, the nobles' reaction, and our role, and we must grow, ebb and flow with it or our kingdom will fall, and the sun will not rise, or it will be fed by the blood of our empire.

Unfortunately for my eyes, I saw a hungry warrior pierce the invisible circles and assault two enemy nobles with his ambition.

A hungry warrior wants to kill and has the skill, has studied, is gifted with rage, strength, but did not spill into life as a noble, so this hungry warrior *will* kill the enemy. To him the enemy is the enemy, and the enemy is a way to spill into the nobility. So he does not dance, he stalks, charges, he brawls, he is a brute. And his noble, the noble from his emperor and homeland, knows of the Hungry Warrior's potential, his prowess.

I saw the regular, motivated and gifted, angry and powerful regular soldier approach the enemy prince; his hunger revealed itself in his straight, unmannered step, a genuine step, a thud, a poised guard, no dance, no posture, no style, a determination in his eyes, the prince's death printed, coded into the hungry warriors' soul, in the veins in his arm, the prince's head resting in the bent crook of his regular right bicep and elbow, a foot and a half of forearm below the fat fist wrapped around the obsidian club that is smiling with its black, sharp, cut-glass smile, waiting to kiss his cheek, his neck, and waiting to put an end to his line. And the prince balks, cannot apply himself to his form, his dance which can work if properly finessed, if not intimidated, if not out of mind, if there is presence of mind.

But the Hungry, the Starving Warrior stepped on his own possible glory.

He threatened to take from that prince the careful strings of victories cultivated by his king and empire, that glimpse of history stored in all he had seen, and the visions of those he had captured, and those they had captured. With one fell-swoop, this Hungry Warrior could capture half as much history as his own noble, but three feet away, had been privy to through his noble and all nobles' sweat.

And too, this would increase antagonisms with the enemy's nation which would be humiliated that this regular warrior captured one of their gifted princes who had reluctantly agreed to this escalated sparring-match-Flower War which still takes time, resources, energy, morale, and fear. And to give up this talent this way could lead to an arrow war where the dead bodies simply stack up, and men endeavor, dedicate themselves to *truly* kill each other. And under the conventions of any war a death is never as valuable as bringing back home a sacrifice still squirming, to see the life drain out of him, to ritualize his death to an exponential experience beyond his lifetime and its reincarnations, influences beyond just his and your experience.

And where I was standing then is where I am standing now.

I circle the imaginary circle around the brilliant warriors asserting our nobility, which I dare not pierce. And I wait. Running from one edge of the circle to the other, looking for someone. Ready to give my lord my teeth if he asks.

As the regular soldier raises his club, he is struck down from behind by his own prince, our own prince, and a crisis is avoided.

We are fighting your princes and ours.

And I wonder if everyone has seen what I have seen or if this imaginary circle is something that they cannot see through or if it is part of the shield that protects their minds from their eyes.

And there is no one to tell. Killing me will shatter my record of the princes' treason, which, of course, will always be there to remind me of the sight. But to not speak pushes the image further into my mind, further into my history, makes me think I saw it when I was young, before I was born, over the shoulder of my father as he climaxed into my mother.

And my claim to fame will be my flayed empty skin tied to the back of a powerful priest of our enemy.

And only then

I will be freed into

the place of the sun does not exist. It is an empty temple, abandoned, an armory of treasons, it is where my skin is flayed, and I will watch my destiny, my crumpled skin tied by my flaccid, dried arms, around the neck of a lord.

There will be no bones hung in front of my house

my father will not get to devour a part of our enemies

instead, this empire is designed to relieve me of my skin, and put me on display in front of a noble's abode, overshadowed by the bigger bones, or shinier bones, thicker bones, malformed bones of the other skeletons in line, where we have been waiting and waiting for the sun to please stop shining, to stop bleeding on us, to stop pissing on us.

In the Flower War in front of me,

we define the outside bubble, based on the wiggles of the standards, the flags of our heroes, our neighbors, the eaters of the food that leads to our crumbs,

and we watch each other tiptoe forward, and while the princes lunge and pounce, I tiptoe into the cold waters of history, I skirt-dance, I girl-dance; it is just like the girl-dance during festivals, and where before I was proud they were enticing us, I could then not be sure they were not mocking us.

and our heroes pass through us to join in the history, to add to, to sculpt the broad strokes of history, to add to the one degree of the single degree that our heroes sculpt the angle of the broad stroke of history.

And there has been some signal, some sign, to let the princes know, to let us know that the bubble has been pierced,

and then the enemy's heroes sift through ours, as if walking through each other, unharmed,

as the nobles pass the lines.

And they are coming for us, the lines have opened for captives, but no prince will be touched.

The first noble, in red and white feathers, looks sated. He is not in his stance. We do not exist in his sights because his gullet is full. He is there to steal a magic sword if we are near a sword and try to stop him, to steal feathers that have not touched the ground. And they are his.

And then my mirror-twins approach.

my mirror-dummies, mirror-zombies, living-dead, dead-living, living-waiting-to-die, missing even glory in that. Enemies like me, doomed to my station in life, covered in maguey war paint.

And the young ones want to fight, like I once did. To really kill. To really battle.

I face an older Second, or Third, or Fourth, like me, just past the ripening age, still not covered in war paint or war mantels. We look into each others' eyes, and we know that we know. And we circle each other, and we exaggerate our moves. I let my shoulder telegraph my overhead strike so that his shield will be there when it lands. I let up as a youngster from my side approaches, and I chase him off, claim this for my own, and he moves, no time to argue, just enough time to look for another capture to latch on to.

Then my twin swings wide to his left, and with his eyes lets me know he will thrust the club at my midsection, and I tell him

the sinking of my heart, the sliding down of my will, the raising of my consciousness, the hardening of my mind, the letting down of my prince, the egret of my regret, the symptom of melancholy,

the twitching of my eye, the laxing of my fist, the quivering of my lip, there is an elasticity to my movement missing, a lower-case "k" to my kill, and cactus, the drooping of my eye and spirit, the white flag of my eyes, the resignation of my soul, the emptiness of my eyes. I open my eyes as wide as I can, and though I block and block and only block, raise my club, too slow, too high, not telegraphing anymore but shouting my intentions by the posture and craning of my attacking arm, the exploiting of my senses, I let him stare into my soul, I invite him to stare in my soul, to spit in my soul, that my fears of going back are greater than his fears.

with the right movement,
that I am ready to be captured. Take me.

Miguel Arteta

Miguel Arteta is the writer and filmmaker who created
STAR MAPS.

Jan 25

Just to think of it, is that it?

All the movies to see
Are in your mouth.
When I'm close like in a close-up
and the sound is turned way up
like a giggle.

And the hours . . .
Your skin must be peeling
passing jokes, drinks, looks, and bills
To buy lipstick or a present
to Forget his face,
Please! Put it away for today,
I know where to find it,
It's tired, It's boring, that's
what that means

Time splits like all the
phone calls I should return soon . . .
And there too lurks a world
so strange, and so common
And it could be mine, will it?

Paste my heart, then, please

Stephen D. Gutierrez

Stephen D. Gutierrez's book *Elements* won the 1997 Nilon Award for Minority Fiction for Elements. His work has also appeared in *The Americas Review, Bilingual Review, Saguaro*.

La Gloria Meets La Helen en la Marqueta and What is Best Left Unsaid is for You

para mi nieta
y todos who might read this in the future and whenever
"Helen, what are you doing?"
"Pues nada, esa, just hanging around."
Like that's what she was doing that day, just hanging around,
looking a little lost and confused in the marqueta.
She didn't look too good.
Especially around the eyes she looked a little sad.
I reached for her arm, but not too much.
"You sure, esa, you okay," I said, barely touching her.
"Yeah, I'm okay, Gloria," she said. "I ain't bad at all."
She looked at me, kind of smiled-mumbled.
Then I let her go.
Because all kinds of people were already looking at us. Al-
ways you get two cholas together talking the old talk you get like
stares, put downs from old times, way back, coming up around you.
So I let her go.
She just walked down the aisle by herself.
She didn't look too good that day.
She looked real skaggy as a matter of fact.
She wore one of those old leather miniskirts black and faded.
Hers looked worse because it had like half the nalgas
worn out with shine and the other half buffed to a mellow black.
I'm a poet, ha?
Or maybe it was the other way around, come to think of it.
Half the nalgas worn out with wear and the other shining
brightly from who knows where.
Ha!
And she went dragging her ass down the aisle, La Helen
did, did La Helen.

On a Saturday night I saw her.
I was just in there for a few things myself.
It was such a change to see her.
From the old days she had come a long way, baby.
Or not such a long way, baby, if you know what I mean.
If you get my drift, you're on to what I'm trying to tell you.
She had sunk real low since the old days.
In the old days La Helen ruled us all.
She was fine, firme, de aquellas.
Un broad that you can be proud of was La Helen in the old days, de veras.
And now she had sunk to this.
A street girl, a hooker on the streets was La Helen when I saw her and when I had seen her before.
A few times before in the years I had seen her.
Always the same old song with La Helen it was.
Barely saying hello to each other we did when it was worse.
Then it got better sometimes.
Then it got worse.
For us all as a matter of fact you might say it got worse.
And better too it did sometimes.
During those years I was on top of the world.
With La Helen on the bottom I didn't pay her much mind.
Not that I had anything bad to say, you know, I didn't.
But just staying on top of my own game, of my own life, if you know what I mean, was enough for me.
I gave her all I could in the old days.
"Helen, how you doing?" I'd say, grabbing her arm in the marqueta.
Or maybe it was outside the church where I'd see her once in a while.
All bundled up in a sweater she'd be.
She'd be freezing like shivering even though it was June.
She'd be on the stuff then, too.
All year she'd be shooting up, walking the streets, starting

up in some program down south, then back on the streets again she'd be for a little while.

La Helen.

She wasn't so bad then for a while.

But I gave her all I could while I could.

Once I even gave her a ride.

So we were carnalas from way back.

La Helen and I go back to the old days in Fresno.

When we were young it was bad.

And now I'm an old faded chola telling my tale.

In the old way I talk I remind myself of myself back then because you wouldn't believe who I am now.

A secretary.

I'm a secretary for a big shot attorney in the city hall in the downtown of Fresno where the gabachos and the Mexicans all clean-cut and cute enter the halls of justice.

Ha!

I seen her sitting here a few times in my flush days.

And I went up to her and put an arm around her right in the middle of everybody.

Sitting down next to her I scooted next to her real tight-like and whispered, "I love you, Helen," in her ear, "you're gonna make it."

But she was too far gone then to do anything for herself.

In and out of rehab she's been all these years.

Sometimes crazy on the streets she's been.

That's after she was crazy with us.

A different kind of crazy I'm talking about here.

When we were young it was fun and dumb.

Now it's all serious and shit.

La Helen comes into my life again on a Saturday night and my life ain't so hot, neither.

I'm divorced.

The viejo left.

He found himself another chick.

What more can I say?

She was good-looking?

Yeah.

She was young?

Yeah.

He's an asshole from way back and I'm better off without two?

Yeah.

No.

I don't know, man.

Only that my life ain't so hot I know for sure now.

Things are different than they were in the old days, I'll tell you that for sure.

Back in the old days we had fun, no matter what.

We went out and partied.

We fucked.

We gang-banged.

Might as well admit it some of the crazy shit I've done in my life, de veras, ese, Mr. Man.

I've stabbed a chick high in an alley.

I've stolen a big wad of cash from an old lady.

I've done all kinds of crazy shit, man, just to pass the time and have fun and be real.

Be real no more is what I can't do.

It's what I find it hard to do now.

I can't smile like in the old days.

They called me La Smiley, but let's not get into that because that's just gonna bring a lot of pain and heartache anyway.

And those are two things I don't need right now, de veras.

I got enough on my mind without more.

But I saw Helen the other day in the marqueta and she kind of sobered me up if you know what I mean.

She was lingering in the potato-chip aisle, looking kind of stupid.

Then I went up to her.

"Helen," I said, "how you been?"
But she barely recognized me really.
Pushing her hair back she looked at me for a long time.
Then she managed, "Gloria?"
Kind of with a crooked smile she had.
She looked on the verge of tears.
Then she crumbled into something else.
Her face just kind of changed, esa.
She looked real bad, real sad.
Standing there in the middle of the Safeway we must have been a sight to see.
Two old cholas from way back greeted each other with a lot of pain between them.
To tell you the truth I left out half the story.
I just couldn't tell it, esa.
It was just too painful.
What we been through and all ain't nice, ain't pretty, ain't for polite ears, you might say.
I took a little college on my way here.
To the marqueta I drove in my Suburu.
A little blue one with a black vinyl top I own.
Says "Glory" on the license plate because I was lucky to get that.
Just told the guy at the DMV, "I want that!"
And when he said yes, kind of smiling and nodding, I thought, "Que chavalo," him in the DMV in his coat and tie, a new kid, a new worker there.
He's Mexican American, or Chicano if he's got any sense.
Handing out our new forms he's all smiles.
And then I go walking out in the night.
I mean from Safeway.
Where I saw Helen that night was on the middle of Blackstone here in the old hometown of Fresno.
She just stood there for a while shaking in front of me like she was ready to crack up.

Then her eyes softened.

Then I reached for her, and she went on her way up the aisle minding her own business.

La Helen, de aquellas, was one fine broad in her day.

Maybe she'll be back one day.

Who knows?

I don't.

And you don't.

Whoever you are reading this story maybe one of these days don't know.

All I want to say, man, is that I saw her, and for like a split second or something we recognized each other or something, again, and the old times come flooding back on me, like in a rush, and I saw my carnala standing in front of me, all torn up and hurting, and I wanted to do something, but I couldn't, because I still carried all that weight from the past, because we loved each other once, we did, de veras, in ways that ain't fit for this story, if you know what I mean, ways that only carnalas and homegirls know about, and I was just left standing there, you know, with nothing to say, no words to say, to my old friend Helen, my carnala, walking up the aisle away from me.

"Wait, Helen," I wanted to say, but that won't work.

In the end I guess we're all alone anyways.

But sometimes I don't feel so alone neither.

I see homeboys and homegirls from the old times around town.

I see them in the parking lots and the stores, buying things, talking, sometimes down and out, sometimes doing real good, too.

We stop and talk, me and the old crowd de aquella tiempo.

We stop and have a cigarette.

We stop and bullshit all day.

Sometimes a minute seems like an hour.

Sometimes an hour turns into a dawn in bed with somebody you don't know.

Because we've all changed so much over the years it's

Stephen D. Gutierrez

hard to keep in touch with who you are.

But they're there in front of me, the old crowd, reminding me of who I was and who I am always.

They're there in front of me laughing and gabbing always, always putting on some big show for my sake.

"Gloria! Long time no see!"

And then some ruca's squealing into my arms, and then some vato's giving me a hug.

It's all right.

These intimate little moments that happen are okay.

Say, last week I ran into somebody from the old crowd at the library.

He was looking into some books on real estate, saying he was going to make a killing on the houses in the West side of town, the fucked up side of town, selling them to wetbacks for way more than they're worth.

Then when I told him, "Sin verguenza, man leave them alone," he told me he was just jiving and didn't know what the fuck he was doing, either.

Just checking out some books on this and that he was.

You see people like that around town, people from the old times getting in touch with their roots.

I mean they're not getting in touch with their roots.

They're just reading or something.

Trying to make themselves better they are.

This is one way to do it.

So you see some vato at the library once in a while checking out a book at the counter.

Or already at the door he is thumbing through his book on the way out.

And then you see each other and you go, "Hey, man, how's it going?" and you start talking for a while about this and that.

Nothing special.

People come up, though.

All these names from the old times float around us in the

moment we enjoy each other's company.

Two sparkling eyes look at me.

They are God's.

My life has been all right, man, not too bad.

And if I wanted to admit the truth I could.

I fucked up.

I fucked up read bad from way back.

And then I fucked up some more.

But I cleaned up my act some, esa, and when you see your Granny walking down the streets say with pride, "That's my abuela, ese, she did some good in her life, she was something."

Say it with pride.

Don't turn away with shame from me, Ruby, who I'm writing this for after all.

You know more than I know what you gotta do to survive.

Be good, be strong, be firmote in the right ways.

Do what you want to do without hurting people, and when you do got to hurt people, do it with style.

I don't know what I'm saying, Ruby.

Forgive me.

She passed by me like a queen in the end.

In the crazy aisles of that store I let her go by me.

La Helen, la ruca más loca de mi barrio Fresno, gathered herself up like a momentous being.

And then she was out the door, Ruby, all fucked up into the night.

Tatiana de la Tierra

Tatiana de la Tierra earned a Master of Fine Arts in Creative Writing from the University of Texas at El Paso. She is the former editrix of the Latina lesbian publications *esto no tiene nombre*, *conmoción*, and *el telarañazo*. Her work has appeared in the *Tropic, Miami Herald Sunday Magazine, Cimmaron Review, Chasing the American Dykedream, Hot & Bothered*, and *Perra!*. Her work is also forthcoming in the anthology *Women on the Verge: Lesbian Tales of Power and Play.*

a latina lesbian activist's survival guide: o, mejor dicho, activism de-mystified, de-glorified & de-graded

it all begins with a driving desire for justice which turns into an untamable vision that seems manageable and practical yet intangible. before you lunge and wreck a decent life (yours), consider some thoughts & tactics from one who lives la radical revolución que algún día se le ocurrió:

• the odds are against you. most likely, you don't have the resources, support, history, or allies that are vital to your plan of acción.

• no matter how pc it is to dig the latina lesbian nation, "they" could really give a shit. "they" care most deeply about "their" advancement, not about you or your agenda or your nada, mi'ja. tokenism is still close to home.

• about those nice anti-racists—if they walk their talk and you don't feel like una decoración on their lapel, use them.

• when you're trying to get into one of those we've-never-seen-a-latina-lesbian-in-this-environment types of situations, expect to do intense legwork that will pave the way for others in the future, but maybe not just yet for you.

• use that grubby white-racist guilt to your advantage.

• if you're working with your latina lesbian familia, don't expect support.

• there really are evil people and some of them are in your community. don't let the greedy, dishonest, lying, classist backstabbing dirty political players alienate you from your dream or from the people who share it.

• for all your merits, you're just una exagerada, a chronic mal-content, a troublemaking escandalosa, an obnoxious gravel in everyone's shoe. the world would be so much smoother if you'd just shut up.

• regardless of how grand your scheme is, it will most likely mean that you'll end up waiting in line at kinko's or office depot to photocopy your earth-shaking documents. brace yourself—they could be out of that "solar yellow" paper you envisioned.

• the most humiliating experience of all: selecting the appropri-ate stamp at the post office. if you hate u.s. flags, wooden ducks, males, buildings & "love" stamps, be prepared to suffer. DO NOT say "fuck" within hearing range of your local postal clerks.

• oh yeah, a few possible side effects: blurry vision, sleep depri-vation, extreme poverty, messy house & burnt food, bureaucratic frustrations, diminished sex life, continual injustice, deteriorat-ing health & no social life to speak of. it's all so grand!

• keep your vision in check. it may all be worth it.

Jail Time for Beginners

The day began with a list of errands: *gasoline, bagels, clinic, protest, photocopies, Eckerd's-film, prescription, step aerobics.* After all that, I intended to come home, sweaty from my workout, and put some eggplant parmesan in the oven while I showered. After eating, I'd get in my king-size bed and flip through channels on the TV, and if nothing inspired me, I'd grab my mystery novel of the week, *Devil's Gonna Get Him,* and read myself to sleep. My day would be that simple.

But it wasn't.

For one thing, I was poor. The business that I'd managed for five years was sold the year before and I hadn't worked since. I had been living off of unemployment and my savings, both of which were just about depleted, and I wasn't exactly looking for a job. I was a writer, dammit, and I was going to cultivate my craft. Which meant poverty.

Most people didn't know how poor I was. I wore emerald earrings, thick Cuban link chains, solid gold bangles and an assortment of gaudy rings studded with diamonds, garnets, sapphires, pearls, amethysts and stones I didn't even know the names of. I sported Christian Dior sunglasses, scented my aura with Oscar de la Renta's *Volupté.* I had kick-ass music, rock, and book collections. I had a Nikon, Bose speakers, a Yamaha stereo, a $50 stapler, a $200 halogen desk lamp, and a decent computer. I still had my health club membership. And I still had a taste for fine food and designer clothes that any employed, vegetarian, liberal, thirty-something lesbian living in Miami would have. I just didn't have the cash.

And so I cringed at the price of a sturdy 30" x 42" piece of cardboard at Office Depot the night before my arrest: $6.49. No way could I afford that! On the other hand, what if I used it so carefully that I could return it the next day, saying that I didn't need it after all? Poverty makes you resourceful, and since I had been plenty poor growing up, I knew how to handle simple survival skills. I bought the cardboard.

I worked by the light of my 25" Mitsubishi. With the cardboard on the floor, I placed continuous sheets of printing paper over the surface and taped all the sheets together. Then, I attached the taped sheets to the edge of the cardboard, and I was ready to make my sign. After using it, I would just remove the paper clips and the makeshift paper sign, return the cardboard, and get my money back.

Or so I thought.

Being unemployed gives you an edge when it comes to civic protests. I was editing a Latina lesbian magazine and working on a series of creative nonfiction stories, which I wasn't being paid for. It's not like I had loads of time on my hands, but then I also didn't have to punch the clock. When I heard that there was going to be a demonstration in front of the Colombian Consulate by Cubans who were incensed because Colombia was negotiating the sale of petroleum to Cuba, I decided that for once, I wasn't going to sit back. I also decided to keep my impending actions a secret from my macha Cuban lover; the Cuban flag dangled from her rear-view mirror and she was as right wing as the rest of them when it came to issues relating to politics on her island. *Comunistas*, she would sneer.

Like many others, I was accustomed to rolling my eyes when Cubans strutted along Miami streets chanting things like *No Castro, No Problem*. There they go again, I would think. But when it came to Colombia, the beautiful country where I was born, I had to draw the line. Colombia, my crib on earth, the place of cumbias, vallenatos, volcanoes, arepas and tiny towns tucked in the mountains, was too dear to me. I wasn't going to let it get slapped around by a bunch of crazed Cubans.

And so I made my sign. It read: *Down with the Cuban embargo*.

The next morning, I filled up my gas tank, as planned,

and bought sesame bagels from the Bagel Emporium in South Miami. Then, I headed to the poor people's clinic in Coconut Grove, where I had an 11 am appointment for a follow-up. I got there early, well knowing the paperwork and waiting routine. The receptionist ignored me. Snotty-nosed kids bolted through the waiting room. *Cristina* provoked the audience. Heterosexuals sat with their arms around each other. A woman in a sleeveless house dress shuffled. Doctors paraded by in their white lab coats. It was 11:30 and the receptionist was still ignoring me.

"Listen," I said, indignant, at a receptionist who obviously wasn't listening. "I have an appointment at noon. Can you speed this up?"

"They haven't found your records, ma'am. You'll have to wait," she replied without looking up.

"What if I come back in an hour?" She shrugged. I figured I could go to the protest, wave my sign around a bit, and be back in time for the doctor.

Okay, it was an ignorant thing to do. There they were, about a thousand demonstrators, all of them revved up. A huge Cuban flag was held by over a dozen pair of hands in front of 280 Aragon Avenue in Coral Gables, the site of the Colombian Consulate. Protesters chanted *No oil for Cuba!* and *Colombia Sí, Gaviria No!* They said things like *Giving Cuba oil is like giving oxygen to Fidel Castro.* Meanwhile, Colombians, who had been advised by the Colombian Consulate to avoid confrontations with the protesters, silently passed out flyers that read *Long live sovereign Colombia* and *Down with the dictatorship of the Cuban exiles!* Network news video cameras were strategically perched around the crowd and police officers roamed the periphery in their blue uniforms. And then I appeared.

Viva Colombia! I chanted, marching with my sign. I wore a brand new cotton t-shirt with *Free Cuba* on the front and I had the Colombian flag draped around me like Superman's cape. The Colombian National Anthem played inside of me. *¡Oh gloria inmarcesible, oh jubilo inmortal!*

And then they creamed me.

In a matter of seconds, the sign was torn from my grip, becoming incoherent pieces of crimson letters scattered at my feet. Suddenly, I was surrounded by flailing arms and bulging eyes. *¡Comunista! ¡Puerca! ¡Puta!* They cursed and screamed at me. And then they pounced on me. A thump to my ribs, a kick to my shin, a bop on the head. They pulled at my Colombian flag, trying to rip it and strangle me with amarillo, azul y rojo, the national colors. I was a fist accidentally thrust into a revolving fan.

So I fought back. Now, I grew up fighting with cousins and siblings and neighborhood bullies, and when it comes down to it, fighting is nothing more than survival instinct. So I belted, punched, pulled, grabbed, grunted and basically, lost all my demure demeanor in public. Unfortunately, a few of those punches landed squarely in the chest of a City of Coral Gables police officer.

And then swiftly, even gracefully, two hairy-armed cops dragged me away from the crowd, lifting me as if I were nothing more than a fluffy teddy bear. "They're the ones who attacked me! Why don't you get them?" I yelled. I was pissed. A group of protesters followed us on the block-long journey to the squad car, continuing with their curses. They swatted at me, smacking the cops instead.

From all appearances, you would think that I was under arrest. I mean, there I was, in the back seat of a police car, locked in. My bottle of Evian was confiscated, as well as my waist pouch and the Colombian flag. The only problem was that no one would tell me what was going on. Cops milled around, glancing at me. One fingered my driver's license. Another spoke into the car radio. One, dressed in blue jeans, a white polo shirt and a baseball cap, got into the front seat. He slid open the bullet-proof dividor a few inches and asked questions without looking at me.

"So what are you doing here? What do you do?"

"I'm a writer."

"A writer, huh? What do you write?"

"Stories." Was this a job interview? He was taking notes. I wanted to say, "I'm a lesbian terrorist and I write cunt stories and I hate men, especially ones like you, and can I please have my bottle of Evian now?" But something told me to play the game. For all I knew, I was being interrogated by an undercover agent from the red squad. *Just be cool,* I told myself.

If things really happened like they did on *The Streets of San Francisco,* they would have had me place my hands on top of the squad car and they would have pat me down. Then, they'd read me my Miranda rights, handcuff me, shove me in the car, and peel off with blue flashing lights, sirens wailing. I would be foaming at the mouth and thrashing about on my way to jail, and once I got there, I would be allowed one phone call and then I would sit behind bars until I was rescued. But it wasn't like that at all.

As the squad car pulled away, I saw the flags and signs from the demonstration dancing in the afternoon wind. I watched Miami through black-tinted folding Ray-Bans. The wind beyond my stifling vacuum-sealed box taunted me. Hair blew. Skirts rustled. Signs quivered. Leaves trailed. A little girl in peach overalls crossed the street in front of me, looking like she might flutter away. A scraggly-bearded man gripped a hand-made sign that read *Soy Balsero, Ayudenme.* Written on corrugated cardboard, the sign moved in the wind. A newspaper vendor cradled a flapping stack of *The Miami Herald* to his chest. Fronds of Royal palm trees whipped, seeming to spiral into the sky.

I thought of a teenage photograph of me standing in the back of a Renegade jeep during a drive through Colombian mountains. My face cut through the gushing wind, my hair flew, and I was ecstatic.

But the wind in Miami, the salty ocean-side breeze, would just have to wait. There I was, a grown woman in the back seat of a squad car, strapped in like a two-year old into a car seat. Thirty-three. That's how old Jesus Christ was when he was crucified. Was this a thirty-something rite of passage? And then I

flashed on one of those rebirthing sessions I'd had the year before. In one life, I had been beaten to death by a small-town mob.
In another, I had been publicly executed. Was this a continuation
of horrid past-life habits? As soon as this was over, I swore to
myself, and as soon as I could afford it, I'd see a psychic, an
astrologer and a rebirther, for good measure. I would confront
my karma.

But first I would have to confront a jail cell in Miami.
Contrary to the zillion jail images that I'd seen on TV all of my
life, I was never actually behind bars. In fact, I never even saw
bars. What I did see plenty of was concrete walls and benches, a
beige steel door, and bullet-proof steel-meshed windows.

And about that one phone call. I did see a public phone
along the wall in the first holding room I was in, but as soon as I
grabbed the receiver, a correction officer yanked me back to the
bench. I eyed her butch hardware with great interest, allowing
myself a brief dyke fantasy, even though she did take my one
phone call away. That gave me more time to think of who exactly I would call. My Cuban lover or my Colombian mother?
Neither would be very sympathetic. *That'll teach you to mess
with Cubans,* my lover would say, laughing. *You've shamed the
entire family,* my mother would say, crying.

Suddenly, I had my image to consider. What would my
family and friends think? How would this affect my Latina lesbian public image? My valiant entry into the protest and the en-
suing mêlée was captured on film. I was the only
counter-demonstrator and I knew that my performance, however
unintentional, was a newsworthy item. I hoped that at the very
least I looked good on film. I had been wearing my bright yellow, plastic carnation earrings, which contrasted dramatically with
my dark curly hair. And my lipstick was fresh and my hands
were adorned with my many gaudy rings. Color coordination
was important to me, even in jail.

I had to use the bathroom, or rather, I pretended that I had
to use the bathroom, hoping to be able to cradle my head in my

hands in private. The officer handed me a wad of stiff white paper. Then, to my surprise, she led me into a large room full of chatty women. Oh oh. *This* is where I had to pee? Prostitutes with wilted hairdos and smeared make up eyed me without halting their conversations. One wore a mini-dress, finely-sculpted bronze thighs, enchanting big breasts. The sort of night woman my lover would whistle at on Biscayne Boulevard at 3 a.m. Suddenly, I was in solidarity with my competition in that room that had two concrete benches along the sides, with stainless steel toilets and a water fountain at each end. I felt like an intruder, like I'd crashed a private party. Was this an opportunity to have deep feminist talks with the girls? To make connections for post-jail sexual encounters? To get manhandled into ecstasy by uniformed female officers? The possiblities were endless.

"You better do your business. I don't have all day," scolded the cop.

No one seemed to care while I pulled down my black Danskin leggings and pink Jockey underwear and nonchalantly peed.

Then, it was back to the solitary bench for me. Back to looking at a public pay phone I couldn't use. Back to a cellophaned bologna and cheese sandwich that appeared out of nowhere. I tried to be well-mannered about the situation. "Can you please tell me what is going on?" I asked the officer stationed by the steel-bolted door. A pink property form and a yellow arrest warrant were my only sources of information.

"Sit down. You'll find out soon enough," she replied. She reminded me of the receptionist at the clinic earlier. Then, without explanation, I was taken into another room and locked in alone with that gummy white-bread sandwich. Is this where they put people when they ask questions?

There was some process involved in what was happening to me, but I didn't know what it was. Couldn't they have designed a brochure explaining the procedure? I fantasized getting out of jail and having the City of Miami hire me to write the text for the prison public-relations pamphlet. *Welcome to the Dade County Public Jail! If you find yourself facing concrete walls behind steel-bolted doors, it means that you are under arrest . . .* Or maybe I could produce a video dramatizing the process, with helpful tips on jail-cell etiquette. *Jail Time for Beginners* would be required viewing of first-time arrestees.

But no such luck for me. I cursed *Hunter* and *Columbo* and *The Mod Squad*. They were all useless as I succumbed to being a jailbird. I thought of the fierce dykes who stood their ground at the women's encampments on nuclear sites. I thought of all that news footage I'd seen on TV with Vietnam protesters, anti-nuclear activists and Black Power crusaders. They looked so fierce while they chanted and pulsed their fists in the air. I had imagined that when they were jailed they would be defiant. They would sing *You can't kill the spirit*. They would laugh at uniformed authority. They would be tough, they would know their rights, they would have massive support on the outside, and they would have colorful stories to tell their grandchildren.

But being in jail is actually very boring. You get put in one room and then another, and then another. You get processed. You get bad photos taken of you. You're fed watery string beans, Spam and Kool-Aid. Your behind gets sore, and you get no answers. Eventually, you get to make your one phone call, and you call your mother, the one person who will put up with you, no matter what.

And then, at some point, you go home. You disconnect the telephone, put on the mellowest music that you have, and take a deep, hot bath with lavender suds. Then, you light some sandalwood incense, get in bed and open the window in the bedroom. The wind travels inside, purifying and soothing you.

And then you say to yourself, *Tomorrow, I'll look for a job.*

Ethriam Cash Brammer

Ethriam Cash Brammer was born and raised in the border community of El Centro, California. He completed his degree in Literature and Creative Writing at the University of California, San Diego. He earned a Master of Fine Arts in Creative Writing at San Francisco State University. He is the translator of *The Adventures of Don Chipote: When Parrots Breast Feed* (Arte Público Press) and has just completed a collection of bilingual poetry *Strange Courage: Que coraje.* He is at work on *Calendarios,* a collection of experimental short fiction.

All-American Canal

The superior court of california county of imperial
is now called to order, ceiling fans wobble above
as spinning blades beat down waves of july heat
bouncing off molded alabaster walls and chestnut
floor-boards which creak beneath black cloaked steps
marching up to a gavel-slap bench of mahogany sweat,
case 1331 the people of the state of california versus,
it all comes back to him in desert vision déjàvu
wearing county issues and staring out the window,
the district attorney of imperial county accuses
the defendant of the following crimes count 1
murder in violation of section 187 of the penal code
on or about april 14th 1989 the said defendant did
willfully unlawfully and with malice aforethought
murder a human being it is, further alleged that
in commission of said offense the defendant used
a deadly and dangerous weapon to whit a knife
it is further alleged, he settles back into his seat
watching legal jargon rise to meet a ceiling fan buzz
as shredded words fall before his eyes like confetti,

he can still see the game on tv, dodgers, padres,
he was with some little friend of some cousin of some
cousin's little friend he just met at the drive-in,
heard you jus got outta the q ése, chino, his voice
heavy mercury swimming in spectrum solder swirls of
i don't want to talk about it, but the vato can't hear it
somehow and keeps on asking dumb-ass questions,
you get that in the pinto ése, pointing with his beer can
at the tattoo of la virgen dressed like a pachuca,
nah, he says, annoyed by the way he keeps staring
at her suspendered breasts and cherub crescent moon,
i got this when i was just a little vato loco like you,
what about the cane ése, what about it, getting mad,
you really need that shit or you jus tryin to pimp,
just trying to pimp shit, he picks up his cane,
slams it on the table, this bitch landed my ass in jail,
count 2 sodomy use of force in violation of section 286c
of the penal code on or about the night of april 14 1989
the said defendant did willfully and unlawfully
participate in an act of sodomy it is further alleged,

so we're out cruising one night a bunch of crazy heads
just looking for trouble tú sabes we roll up on this park
over on northside and bam out of nowhere
all these 19th street fuckers are on top of us
and some puto is breaking my knees with a baseball bat,
the kid's eyes get so big they can hear cool breaths
quivering over the silver top of his sweaty beer can,
they grab me by the hair así mira holding my head up
making me watch them kick the shit out of my carnal
then that pinche güey with the bat takes a swing
at his head, he closes his eyes, downs his beer,
the pigs show up of course lights sirens y toda la onda
cholos scatter like cucarachas leaving me there
with two busted knees and a cuate with his head cracked
open like a cantaloupe pero sabes qué that ain't even
the crazy part because when the pigs get out the car
they arrest me got ten years and don't even know
what the damn charge was all i remember is watching
them zip up my homey as they poured my legs
into the backseat, so what're you gonna do now ése,

what can i do i got a record i got a limp i got no job
who the fuck's going to hire me, there's a hush,
he stares at the boy and shakes his head realizing
words have never worked for people like him,
and he thinks language is like a dozen rose tattoos
others can see red pedals but he feels only thorns,
so in the lock-up he learned to occupy his silence,
sabes qué carnal i really admire you ése you're legit
a real veterano not like all those other punk-asses,
he shakes his head again, you fucking deaf güey
10 years in chino ain't no way to spent your youth,
yeah but you're og ése you been to the Joint y todo,
you think that's something to be proud of, yeah,
you want to know what it's like to go to prison ése, yeah,
you really want to know what it's like, yeah,
he whips out a filero, sticks it under the kid's chin,
on your knees bitch, what, on the floor i said,
what're you doin ése, he pushes him down,
holds the blade to his throat, a free hand fumbles
with a belt buckle, and a knife penetrates the skin,

count 3 kidnapping in violation of section 207a
of the penal code it is further alleged, chín chín chín,
panic breath stuffs the body into the trunk, qué hiciste,
blood gushes through razor seams like crude
pumping out of punctured oil pans, he spirals down
the interstate, yuma, once in arizona he can cross over
to san luís, sell the car, and buy some time,
what about the body ése, he pulls off the freeway
where the all-american canal cuts beneath i8 east,
amber lamplights drain upon canal sides as elevation
drops deafen the sound of his heart, chín chín chín,
white water rush is all he hears when opening the trunk,
and he never sees the water district worker parked
in his truck on top of sand dunes, radioing homebase,
as he pulls that bloody rag to the canal's edge,
before he knows it the desert is blooming with siren red
and violet light, in the courtroom, he doesn't even listen
to the legal exchange, just sits mutely, watching guilty
enter as the plea and with that familiar gavel slap
he returns to the silence he never knew how to leave.

Omar Castañeda

Chapter 24 - Excerpt from *Islas Coloradas*

Gary cannot comprehend the exquisite pleasure he feels in just watching the activities of the festival and in his comfort in resting against Shun Oiboysh. It is simply too good to understand; it is too good to endanger with understanding, though it crosses his mind that he might have gotten more than a cure in the fig drink.

Her arm is draped lazily over his shoulder, so that he is nestled under her arm as they both lie in an enormous hammock on a dais that overlooks the center. He can now see that the village has many more huts than what he first thought when hanging paralyzed under the community hut. Some are just visible on the pathways winding through the jungle and leading back to the center, which now, at least, acts as the cultural center, the business district. As leader, Shun Oiboysh's hut is here, as is the main campfire and what is effectively the theater for judicial audiences. There are circular markings around the dais on which the two of them now swing, at ease in the gentle rocking of the yellow, black, and red weave. The ends of the hammock are tied to posts on either side of the dais, which is really no more than a raised mound in front of Shun's hut.

Gary gathers all this by watching a few of the women make formal requests to Shun Oiboysh. The two of them first sat in the hammock upon her return from her hut. She had replaced her simple white loincloth with a finer, white tunic laced with gold threads and hemmed in a gold crosshatch design. Gary enjoys the spectacle before them, the strength exuded by Shun, her beauty, the warm deference the villagers show her. Women squat on their haunches in the marked circles and make their entreaties. Others wait in the outermost concentric circles. As one finishes, the others move to the next inward circle to thus await their turn to speak. When Shun has finished with all the requests, she signals for everyone to rise. She herself rises to proclaim this, then nestles back with Gary.

She pulls him into her arms and kisses his temple. "Eoyde bwemoysh e dwubidtwudnoysh," she says, all smiles.

She touches Gary with such ease and gentleness that he begins to think that he has always lived here, that all those images of some odd place called Clowerston, all the images of a strange band of guerrillas, are really nothing more than hallucination. One not terribly pleasant. This is where he has always lived, where he was born and raised and, long ago, in the misty past, where he had learned to love Shun Oiboysh. They have been in love since time immemorial, since the very first tree rose free of the jungle floor to stand boldly into air, verdant wings outstretched, branches full of luscious fruit.

Gary leans forward and kisses her lips.

She presses into him and then pulls back. Her hand indicates the village. "Ishtzemoysh eligwri kwi esh shoybwrebubudzoy." By the end of the sentence her hand has moved to place a finger on Gary's chin. "Ishtze fuishtze ish in pwedtzi pwede tze," she says, her index finger twirling in the air to indicate everything around them, then she moves her hands to indicate all of Gary. "U pwedtzi pwoydkwi ish il dzue dzi noishtzri Shinoyde dzi Emoyd." She finishes by indicating the heavens.

Her words remind him that, in fact, Clowerston is anything but a dream, and yet there is something tantalizingly familiar about her words and about his being here. He is certain that he will reach a point of understanding her even if he does not understand the words. He consciously decides that, rather than attempt to capture each word and understand each sentence as a proper sentence, he will allow his ears to become flexible, tolerant, his eyes to become receptive and holistically capture meaning in gestures and context. He will understand in abstract ways, osmotic ways.

Thus, her smiles and expressions tell him that he is, regardless of the specifics of her words, part of what is going on.

Together with her intonation of the strange words, they say that he is not only a part of the village, but a part of the heavens and sky, and a part of the cosmic forces that govern this village. Her obvious happiness, an effulgence in her eyes, signifies that he is welcome in all ways.

This interpretation is so satisfying to Gary that he further decides that if any of her words come to develop their own specific meanings, such as what happened with her name, then so be it, but that he will merely enjoy the larger meanings and, of course, her signs of pleasure with his participation. He will allow this very special world he has stumbled upon to come to him through the pores of his skin, if that is the only way it can. He will not even try to determine exact meanings, or demand that correspondences be so tight; instead, he will let words and images settle like silt in the river of his subconscious until there's enough to form a distinct sandbar on which to ground understanding. In this way, understanding swells upward into consciousness, rather than as the usual deconstructing from consciousness. This new philosophy feels like what he has always looked for, it is so comforting.

Around him, the festival is for the longest time nothing more than starts and stops of music, bells and woodwinds, and the bustle connected with hawkers of food, casual bartering and selling of skins, bones, carvings and the like. Immediately after Shun's formal speaking from the dais, the festival changes little. Yet slowly, as if guided by some unspoken word passing extra-sensorially between the villagers, the people begin moving into cliques. Gary notices that the women still wear white loincloths, but that the men and boys now have loincloths of varying colors. The older men wear black and red loincloths with red leis around their waists. Prepubescent boys seem to have no order in their coloring, wearing black and red, blue and red, gray and pink, or single solid colors. They also wear more than one garland, with some around their waists and some around their necks. A few even have bracelets of flowers around wrists and upper arms. Out of the mild chaos, a line forms of young men, wearing solid red loincloths and tight red leis around their necks from which hang large fuchsias like pendants: the blossoms hang up-side down, their pistils red and protruding between the purple and crimson petals. Each of these young men has his hair pulled tightly into a pony-tail. Gary glances around to notice that males and females wear their hair a little longer than shoulder-length. Unlike most Coloradans, their hair is wavy.

"Ekwishtzetzi," Shun says, patting her lap for him to lie down on.

Again, there is a comfort which seems like a covering over him and Shun. Lying there in her lap, however, the idea begins in his head that this aura of comfort is not just around the two of them, but it is a cloak over the entire village. He first sees it in the way the line of young men moves delicately in and out of the women, swallowing up the other males as it passes. At last, it is a full-fledged snake coiling gently around the excited women, who reach out to the males, old and young alike, strok-ing them with the lightest of touches, in the way Shun Oiboysh strokes Gary's face and arms as he rests against her. There is something of the hypnotist in all of the women. They have some magic in their gazes. Their hands undulate as in Balinese dance movements to lull the serpent moving among them. It is a dance of joy. It is a celebration of physical acceptance and of physical contact. It is a bewitching and a taming. Even the youngest boys are part of this snake; even the youngest girls are saplings in the overall forest of women, the roots of which the snake winds through. The music of woodwinds becomes the call of birds above the colubrine dance; the high drums and rattles become the sounds of twigs snapping below; the bells and chimes together are a morning mist rising from the jungle floor. Everything and every-one is the sound of Nature working toward some balance of forces, both terrible and sublime.

Gary is more relaxed than he has ever been. The dream steps of the dancers, the music and the smell of meats and nuts combine with Shun's constant petting to repeat the illusion that he has always lived here in this village, that he has never been elsewhere. His home is here.

The snake slides between the women several more times until the girls lead the boys to sit along the clearing. The snake of men moves languorously through the remaining women and then they, too, break away and sit around the clearing. All of them look up at Shun. She moves to stand, forcing Gary to sit up.

She speaks to the whole congregation, only this time, her voice is hushed and solemn throughout. She speaks not in the rhythms of a political leader, or of adjudicator, but in the somber rhythms of moral discourse, of sacred narrative. It fits perfectly with the whole thaumaturgic dance. Gary thinks that she must be saying something about the greater spirituality of all of them. The villagers stare happily up, imbued with light, yet with a sober respect and love for the interconnectedness of all things. When Shun finishes with arms outstretched, there is a meditative humming from all of her people.

Gary watches as the villagers stand and ritually hug each other. Shun moves him in front to hug. Others, men and women, come near him in their turn and hold their bodies intimately to his. In each, he feels an uninhibitedness that is both arousing and frightening. The frankness is exhilarating, the intimacy shocking to his upbringing. Men and women hold him and then move to the next person. This feeling does not change when he is hugged by a man or woman, as if sexuality were the same to these people, as if they had an awareness of flesh that he has only glimpsed in secret flashes, flashes that have come less and less as he has grown older. He knows that the very secretiveness of the flashes makes them frightening. It somehow implies that there ought to be a radical change in his world. It indicates that he has learned everything wrong, that all his world of sexuality and of relationships has been based on falseness, on someone else's ideas of them. He knows that fear is a glimpse of a collapsing world; fear is the inability to see what may possibly arise from the ashes; and fear makes a terror out of the invisible.

Gary becomes aware that the villagers are staring at him. They are looking at him with pity, as at something sad and unfortunate.

"What?" he demands, now even more frightened that they can read his mind.

Shun, who descended into the congregation for the ritual of hugging, breaks through to ascend the dais. She takes his hand. "Noy shopwumoysh kwi ishtzebwesh kwoyn muidzoy. "

Gary backs up—which is really down—the opposite side of the dais. "What? What have I done?"

She keeps his hand in hers. It is a current of electricity through him. It numbs his fingers and wrist.

"Sh," she says. "Sh."

Gary gasps. He can see that the others behind her are looking at him with open curiosity. Their faces show sympathy, but he does not want sympathy—the idea is insulting!—unless they can actually read his mind. Unless he has done something wrong. He feels suddenly cut away from the ground, the earth; he feels his feet lift off the dais into air. But Shun's strong fingers hold him down and play on his flesh as if she were touching some outer shell that he cannot see. He is transfixed by her mime-like movements. According to these, there is a shape to his invisible husk. For a stupid second, Gary imagines that he has been captured by hippies or Southern Californians who sailed across the waters on a raft made of avocado shells and all-natural yogurt containers.

As if sensing this dumb turn of mind, Shun stands with arms akimbo. The ridiculous image dissolves. Instead, Gary looks into Shun Oiboysh's eyes and sees there a genuine concern, genuine affection. Her hand waves out behind her and the bells and music strike up again. The others proceed from one to the other with their embraces so that he and Shun are effectively left alone.

The purpose of the hugging is evidently to embrace in abstract terms something crucial, something deep and necessary. Gary knows he is missing whatever is passed between them as their bodies press together. It is something so clear to them, so obvious to their perceptions that all of them stopped and stared at him, as perhaps one might stare at someone suddenly discovered to be missing the mental ability to perform some simple task. It is not a stare of condescension—that had been his first interpretation, his defensiveness, under the initial flood of eyes. Really, they had stared with a kind of self-surprise, surprise at themselves for not having noticed earlier and for having their own assumptions proven wrong about who and what he is. He can learn! he wants to shout. He wishes he could know exactly what Shun first said upon breaking through the villagers to take his hand. He wants to tell them that he is willing to learn, to change.

Both of them, it seems, now are at a loss as to what to next.

"I don't know what's going on."

"Kwelmitzi."

Her reassuring breath lets loose the pirates of tension in his shoulders and he closes his eyes.

"Bin," she says, deciding on a course for them. She pulls him by the hand and takes him down through the villagers and across the clearing to the ladder of her hut. She points upward. "Shobwi."

Gary is unsure of himself. All his body says "imminence," "danger."

She wiggles her fingers to imitate climbing legs. "Shobwi, shobwi." She urges him up the ladder by pushing under his arm.

"Up?"

"Noy tzuinish muidzoy."

He ascends, but not without casting a glance at the others in the clearing. Thankfully, they are all involved with their own rituals, their own males. He surprises himself to discover that "they," in this place, means women.

Ethriam Cash Brammer

Autumn Plows

The world goes silent when he realizes he has come
to the end, huuulllaw, wretching over bended knees
as dust settles around a white pick-up truck, come on,
the driver barks, ya didn't have that much ta drink,
his guts spill into the ditch below like soiled wash water
from a tin pail, what did you do, he asks himself,
what the hell did you do, huuulllaw, spectra bubbles
mingle with the copper stain of a setting october sun
floating on jaundiced water and green philangi waves
as he feels himself sink into soft earth embankments
and hears voices resound from times not long before,
you did it didn't you, oh my god, you, really did it,
he didn't say a thing, not one word, fearing the slightest
dubious intonation might give rise to the suspicion
of his captivated audience, for at that age,
in that locker room, where those boys rattled
like flimsy metal doors, all he had to do was smile,
measuring acutely the corners of his mouth
as they rushed him through the door with high-fives
and canine cheer, you did it, oh my god, you really did it,

but now he watches tractors snail across night-shade campos, silver plows churn ash and shaft and wet with tic-toc lunar regularity, purging his wretched torso into a drainage ditch with sulfur bromide heaves, i never thought it would be like this, he whispers as circular blades rake his mind and dust-cloud trails lead him back to her white hacienda with spanish tile, where humongous marbled bullhorns hang mounted over a chestnut leather sofa covered by woven cotton blankets brought back after a day trip to algodones, my dad found those in the desert, he quickly replaces the sharktooth arrowheads and flowering sand-dials he had just excavated from layers of crystalized soot, she hands him a beer, her parents are in laughlin for the weekend so she asked her best friend's boyfriend to bring him over in his pick-up truck, but when polite conversation drowns into mtv chatter she bobs up and threads her way across the room, each stitch pressing navajo carpet beneath her needle-point shoes, let's go for a walk, she says,

golden girasol skies grow dark while thinking
about all those late night telephone conversations
when they would talk about classes and tests, about
people and parties, about anything and everything,
until simply falling asleep, drooling over the telephone,
have you ever done it, he asks, hearing shame
crack in her voice like the sun sweeping desert floors
after a late april rain, yeah, she says, her mumbling
hollowed with degradation as she tells him she once
thought guys only liked her for as long as it took to open
and close their zippers, have you, and he thinks about
lying to her, but doesn't, because he can't lie to her
like he lied to the others. because she means more,
and he wants to be more, more than a macho,
more than a muchacho, no, he says, then explains,
i once went out with this one girl in seventh grade
and the guys started saying stuff, but you never said
it wasn't true, no, and now it was his turn to feel guilty,
knowing he had wanted to be something different,
but that's just the way guys are you know,

they continue their walk along the embankment where pig-pen air smells of gamey meat and tractors turn up earth in clotted rows until they finally reach the fieldside haystacks, it's beautiful, she whispers, purple cocopa peaks burn in flames of cirrostratus amber rings as thunder pounds in the cavern behind his ribs, she takes his hand, begins to stroke it gently watching egrets emigrate in feather puff flocks across pyrotechnic horizons, are you cold, she asks, he hasn't noticed his body trembling, until her long painted nails kiss the back of his neck, her tongue runs along the ridge of his collar, and her fingers liberate silver buttons from his fly, popping open, one by one, she takes him into her hands, and helps him find her lips, huuulllaw, he feels himself shrinking when pulling up his pants and he stops to look at her for the first time, she lies on her back, on a bale of hay, her body is completely naked, her hair slacken straw strewn over fresh alfalfa, violet blossoms hide behind rigid cheekbones, a skeletal chest, her hips, cold, stone,

and he realizes he had scarcely pulled his pants down
to his knees and never took off his plaid cotton shirt,
when she gets up to dress, he turns away, watching
nightcrawler headlights cut through high-beam
dust-clouds as tractors plow through paths of silence,
we should probably be getting back now, he says,
they must be wondering where we are, he starts
walking back to her house without even turning back
to see if she follows, just trying to leave her image behind,
what the hell got inta you, the driver snaps again,
i've been honkin for damn near 10 minutes now,
his haunts subside behind the pick-up, engine roar,
i don't get you kid ya'd think you were allergic ta beer
or ta pussy or both, he feels his body disintegrate
into cracks of grease-stained buckseats because
the driver's wry smile tells him that he knows exactly
where he was and he knows exactly what he was doing,
and perhaps that is the most difficult thing for him
to accept, for after he had done it, after he had
really done it, he didn't want anyone to know.

Miriam R. Sachs Martín

Miriam R. Sachs Martín was previously published in *New to North America* (Burning Bush Publications), *Paginas Tortilleras* (the newsletter for Ellas en Acción), and *Free to Be* (the official San José gay pride magazine), and will be included in the forthcoming anthology *Sinverguenzas*. She produces *Fierce Words Tender,* an open mic for women. She was born and raised in East San José, California.

Mixed

Tell me you're a woman. Convince me. Dime que eres mujer. Show me how you believe it, how you feel it, how you live it. Sing your song to my willing ears and I will believe you.

I don't give a fucking shit what you got down your pants. I don't care what you were born with, I care who you have become.

Tell me that you are a man. Convince me that you crave the slow sensual thrust of lovemaking as cockfucking. Place my fingers on the man's pulse that beats behind your eyes, and sketch out for me your man's hips, your man's ass. I will believe you.

I don't give a fuck what you can show me that's down your pants. Convince me you are who you say you are and then don't bother me with evidence stating otherwise.

Tell me what you are. Believe what you are. Show me you believe. Tell me your name. Tell me. And I'll believe you. Go ahead, and dare it.

And if you tell me that you are both a man and a woman, that you can fall asleep at night tenderly clutching the rounded swells of your breasts, and wake up in the morning with the physical need, like a need to smoke or shout, to bind them down and revel in flat and hard beyond butch—into manly—I'll believe you. And if you tell me that you tried on your mama's high heels as a boy but are now confused by your desire to own combat boots, that you ARE theater and live the dual face of that mask, if you tell me that you wish you could shave off your dick and balls, that you want to traipse around in a leather jacket and a tutu, I will believe you. I will back you. Tell me it hurts to decide. I believe you. Tell me everybody wants you to decide. I'm on your side. Tell me how everyone's hassling you to leap the fence; shit or get off the pot, stand up and take it like a man or spread your legs and put up with it like a woman, tell me that none of your lovers will understand and embrace that you run

97

the gamut from North to South and back again . . . I believe you.
I believe you. I believe you. And you know what else—I got
your back.

Tell me. TELL ME. Open your heart and let it slither,
slide, stamp, punch, roar, parade, prance, sing it's way on out.
Tell me you are mixed. Mixed. Mixed. Sugar love, darling asshole,
friend of my gender and mind of my heart. Tell me about you.
Your shoe collection, your wardrobe, your life and pain and eyes
that blow the current continuum right off the charts. Tell me about
you. Tell me about being mixed. And you know I'm'a tell you
about me.

Being mixed isn't as elusive as it seems. I can trace you
my people with my eyes closed—to Cuba, Russia, Poland. I can
show you the cunt I was born with and the dick I strap on when I
wanna fuck. I can point out my white skin and blond hair, trill
my rrr's, or cook you a mean black beans and rice—I'll show
you my list of the men I slept with before, the women I sleep
with now, and tell you my fantasies of cock and rape and power
that have been here all along. I can show you pictures of my
clothes from little rich girl fairy princess to thirteen-year-old
daughter of a single parent, working before and after school to
help make ends meet. Need I mention that I'm only five foot
one, weigh 117 pounds, am 23 years old? Need I mention that
being mixed has both the cacophony and harmony of specific
musics, smells, foods, people? That hetero and queer do **not** create a middle ground of *bisexual,* nor do Cuban and Jewish cancel
each other out to become *mixed heritage.* It really isn't that elusive at all, this need to create something safe, and genuine, and
even joyful from the "No"s, the "You can't"s, and the cries of
"Traitor!" Being mixed is about taking that no, and making something of it, that No that says if I am Jewish I can't possibly be
Latina, if I get down with the boys, I can't be queer, and since
my Mom owns three houses now, I can't have possibly been
working since I was eleven. It's about taking that No, and nibbling

Miriam R. Sachs Martín

at it like the shell of a nut, holding the No all hard and stubborn
in my hand and picking at it until it falls apart to deliver the rich
brown edible stuff inside. It's about building a sweet little cot-
tage on the fence that separates one identity from the other, it's
about sketching together a whole from many mismatched halves,
and creating a multiplicitous identity as a beautiful garment from
what others call rags, and making a place to lay my head in the
landmine spiked battleground of cultural difference. Being mixed
isn't as elusive as it seems. Being mixed is being fierce. Being
mixed is being brave. Being mixed is making your fucking home
on the split that people want you to run from. Being mixed is
making do. Being mixed is making something lovable out of other
people's leftovers.

Luis Alfaro

Luis Alfaro is a poet, playwright, activist, recipient of a MacArthur Genius Award, and director of Los Angeles' Mark Taper Forum's Latino Initiative.

Deseo Es Memoria

The night after Julio's memorial service I went to the video store and rented an old gay porn tape. I think it was called *Aspen Ski Weekend II*. In it, a beautiful blond guy, who looks like no one I know, gets fucked by everybody in the ski lodge. He sort of half-smiles throughout the video like maybe he's done this just a *few* too many times. Think of Carol Channing in *Hello Dolly!*

They all had that 1970s-porn, pimples-on-the-butt look. Imperfect perfection, I call it. I mean, they were cute and all, but they had that *done-it* look. Lost innocence. A resigned contentment. A grin that says, *Yeah, I give up. Just do what you want with me.* And life says, *My pleasure, motherfucker.*

When I went to bed, all that I could remember about the video was a bouquet of roses that was strategically placed next to the action. In every scene the roses seemed to magically appear within the frame of each thrust and moan. When I should have been paying attention to the big cum shot, my eyes instead caught sight of that beautiful bouquet of red to the left of the improvised sling. And, of course, not a condom in sight. That night I dreamt that everything beautiful was wrapped in condoms. Cocks and roses, all in condoms.

The next day I was reading the Falcon Video newsletter and I found out that Alan Lambert, a cute if not overly eager bottom, had committed suicide in his native Canada. I'd always had a crush on Alan Lambert because he made porn look so easy. He seemed to know his paces, gliding from one position to another like Esther Williams underwater. I'm almost positive he came to porn by way of a gymnastics career. When he mounted a ten-inch dildo, you could almost see Alan's lips mouthing off, in denominations of twenty, his earnings for the day.

In a ten-page document left behind to Falcon Video, he listed a number of important reasons for his self-demise at the old gay porn age of twenty-six. Chief among them was his fear

101

of getting older. He stated that his body was at peak physical condition and that he could not see himself in any other way. This from a man who wasn't even HIV-positive.

The last time I talked to Julio was at the French Market Place. I was meeting a date for breakfast. Someone who looked like Alan Lambert. Julio was walking slowly around the restaurant, out of breath, and looking perpetually chemotherapy-tanned. A few heads turned, but most pretended not to see him. My date arrived and he kissed me on the *cheek*. I'd already begun to imagine how I was going to throw him over my brand-new black lacquered desk and fuck him until he said, *Ooh, talk to me in Spanish.*

Julio came by and he kissed me on the *lips*. I introduced him to my date, who was rippling muscles in a cute little outfit from BodyMaster. Julio told us about how he had just started steroids. His doctors were going to try and give him an ass again. It seems that the virus had taken it away. My date never recovered from the memory of the kiss that Julio had given me. He kissed me on the *cheek* and never called.

At Julio's memorial service his mother got up and told a roomful of queers that his family did not support his lifestyle. That they never went to his art shows. That they did *not* support his lifestyle. That they did not know him the way we knew him. They only knew him as a *wonderful, caring, sweet person.*

Well, I want to reclaim a little history right now and tell you that I knew Julio. I knew Julio as a queer Latino-Filipino. I knew Julio as an artist. I knew Julio's artwork. I also knew Julio as a *wonderful, caring, sweet person.*

I know blood is thicker than water, but I want to say *fuck you* to his mother. I am getting fed up with straight people. Not only do they try to ruin our lives, they try to ruin our deaths as well.

The other day I was driving down Sunset Boulevard in Beverly Hills and I saw a gigantic mural on the Playboy building. It had a picture of a little boy playing with a handgun and it said, *Save the Children, Stop the Violence.* Well, I want a billboard on Sunset Boulevard with a picture of Julio playing with a handgun. I want it to say, *Save the Children, Kill Your Parents.*

En memoria de Julio Ugay.

Miguel Arteta

Feb 11

Complainin not Entertainin . . .

What a world, dick, pussy and a hairy ass, pimples and
deformed skin, loud noise, water and Life and Death, Pain,
coincidence, shit, piss, wow, lose no rhythm, no spelling,
fatness, picking nose, pornography, illness, black stories
told by whites, letters to people we don't care about, Grins
for no one, many cities not visited, secrets kept from loved
ones

shame burning in our throats, fathers that don't care for their
children, contaminated water, bad bad luck, repetition,
analness, red bloody veins

picket fences, dead trees, fat cats, humiliation from wimpy
strange folks, potential world war, earthquakes, bankruptcy,
bad breath, sleepy eye gunk, filth in your teeth, ingrown nails,
stand offish neurotic friends, many broken hearts,

alienated relatives suffering, dead whales, suicidal potential,
armed robbery, contract negations that go forever, losing love
needing more, grunting

full moons alone, no sex, little laughter and sleeplessness

Stop!

SMILE

Tony Diaz

Houston Is A Hot, Wet Octopus

Felix Navida. I could still smell the heat when I woke. That dead-sweat, burnt-feather, salty inferno stalkin' me out of my nightmares just like it stalkt me in.

I rolled out of the damp mattress, buckled 'round my waist the strap studded with two rows of sharp nails, the strap I hang over my head while I sleep, put on my black clothes, dressed in the fresh dark, the soft dark, under the hot triple-X-Mas moon.

'Twaz the night before X-Mass in H-Town and there weren't any Angel Fucks or Ghost Fucks to save anybody from The Head of The Dog. And The Invisible Hand had ordered me to give some unlucky bitch-of-a-son his wings.

Outside the Third Ward house, that Gene Fuck was, holdin' open the rear door of a four-door Bonneville, early 80s, when Bonnies were still big. He made some crack about my beauty rest. I slipped inside the Bonnie and caught a whiff of sulphur—that Gene Fuck sweatin' bullets. You can't hallucinate someone like that Gene Fuck. He wore a bulletproof vest over his bare chest, black zippers all over his parachute pants, hidin' the pistola in one, the switchblade in another. And still, he got the Christmas Tonfa in his right hand, the red, white, and green streamers flailin' at the end, him jinglin' the bells on the handles with every step I took.

That Arthur Fuck, dressed all in black too, was sittin' behind the wheel, staring straight, wearin' a pair of sunglasses even though it was dark—slippin' into the role. We had the windows rolled down, takin' H-Town head on, not ones to let our air be conditioned. And like this, we drove off to our little Christmas party to pass out the presence of The Invisible Hand.

Let me make the plain and simple plain and simple.

There is the law for you. And there is the law for crimes. Under the hyper-capitalism, The Invisible Hand, The Man unleashes

The Head of The Dog to control the crime interest rate.

And The Dog has three heads, and each head has three men. At this time, the three heads of the dogs were The Blacks, The Vietnamese, and we Brown.

The lowest groups in the social order always battle to get on The Dog. The new group pushes another group off The Dog, and once you're Off, you and your kind move up. By right, The Blacks should've been Off two or three groups before, but they were left on—only The Hand knows why. Or how. And then the changes slowed, evaporated into promises, nextimes. The Germans, the Italians, the Irish had been brilliant on The Dog, but they'd been on only a short time, compared to us three, so that we were getting to grumblin' about that fact, and thinking how sometimes, when you get close enough to steal a look, The Hand looks very vulnerable, and we feel very mean. But The Man thinks of everything. One of The Invisible Hand's Yellow Haired helpers let slip that WE, the Browns, could be the next ones Off, if this job went right. And I was not going to get in the way of that.

So it was with great joy that we drove onto West Gray— the perfect name for one of H-town's smaller tentacles, nice then bad, run down, built up, mall-white, then black, then gray, all in the same mile. And all those fuckin' trees. Everywhere, H-town's jungle days poke through its concrete suit, tree trunks pop through the sidewalk, grass wiggles out the cracks.

Every traffic light was flashin' green, a little chaos creatured by one of the other Heads of the Dog. Fucks were stoppin' at the intersections to watch each other scratch themselves. Arthur Fuck stopped behind two rows of cars at this light and damned us next to these two pale Fucks in a jeep with Maine license plates and the air conditioner on. I stared at the Pale Fucks and smiled like I had a clown mask on, smiled wide and waved again. They looked straight at the light, tried to ignore me. Genio and Arturo caught on. All three of us stared and smiled. The driver corner-of-the-eyed us. He turned, checked us out, then tapped Passenger Fuck who turned. They smiled at us and waved. I signalled at the driver to roll down the window. He did and said, "Merry Christmas."

I said, "Hey, Friendly. Do you think I'm friendly or somethin'?"

"What?"

"Do you think I'm friendly or somethin'?"

"Hey, you guys waved first."

"None of us waved. Did you wave?" I said to Gene who shook his head "no."

"I sure as hell didn't wave," Arturo said. "Only faggots wave."

"Are you two trying to be friendly or something?" I said. "Hey, fagboy. Do we look friendly? Do we look like faggots?"

"Sorry, guys," Friendly said. "I didn't mean anything by it. We're sorry. We weren't looking for trouble."

They took off. We sped up behind them and tailgated them. They sped up, we kept up. They were coming to another light with two cars in front of us. When they started to slow down, the front of our car was touchin' their trunk, so Driver Fuck grew some balls and changed over to the wrong side of the street. It was two lanes on both sides, and there was only Christmas stragglers on either side, so the two cars comin' at them blocked us off and they turned. Arthur pulled an "S"-swerve and kept going straight on our path, us laughin' together. And now I laugh because back then I thought—it came to me—that that was just the way some people were picked and that was how some people got away—luck.

Along the pretty part of West Gray, angels hung from the light poles next to the palm trees, the palm trees with their nests of flying roaches that'll blot out the sky some day. Candy canes swung, glittered like they were sweatin'. I glittered too. Houston glittered. It was July in Christ Mass. Roman Candles crashed into Kreshes, shot off Easter Bunny heads. M-80s in your stockings. Put bandages and first aid on your X-Moss list, you Fuck, and check it twice.

The Bonnie swerved onto Shepherd, down the lanes of the valley of the octo-guts to the underpass where Allen Parkway fucks Kirby, luscious Kirby with large houses, big trees, little parks in front of Fucks' Houses, little address markers sticking out of the big squares of grass, stickin' up like grave markers. Hot casas lit up with Kurst Mas lights and lights and lights, so much frosting, so much money, so close to the street you thought any day of the year you could just walk in carollin'. Me Fuck, that Gene Fuck and that Arthur Fuck pulled into the driveway in our hundred-horse-powered open slay. And we were reekin' from sweat. We reeked like smoked ox. Smoked ox that could smoke back.

The driveway sloped down, cut a few chips into hell, the cul-de-sac snaked in front of the steps leadin' up to the patio leadin' to the tall house with the smilin' windows, all lit up with little red, blue, and green lights, and the many Merry Christmas trees. In front, a limo was running, a pendejo chauffeur waiting, holdin' open the limo door. We pulled up and got out so easy.

The year I spent casing H-Town, markin' it, visitin' its dojos, churches, country clubs, night styx, gauging which way it sprayed its kloud of inc, I suspected our little christenin' would take place in the part of town with the brick wall around it. But this house made more sense. With its pillars in front, orange flags where the concrete from the drive ended and the manicured grass started and lifted the house up on a hill like it was sittin' on a covered up batch of H-Town jungle waitin' to spring free. It made sense.

Pendejo chauffeur said hello and merry Christmas to us with his Russian accent. That Arthur Fuck told him "Merry Christmas!" then kicked him in the balls and gave him the knee to the bent-over face. We were all laughin' too hard for Arthur to shove that Russian Fuck into the limo proper. His black Russian boot was left stickin' out. And when Gene saw this, he pointed at it and got me to laughin' all over again at his boot, and at Arthur's Christmas boot, which is what he kept saying, "Merry Christmas—Boot!" Gene jumped inside the limo and pulled Boot into the dark.

We three kings trotted up the stairs to steal back our gold. Up to the patio which is higher than the cars, but level with Kirby, and I wondered if this mutherfucken pharoah ever imagined just how nice a tomb he'd built. And speak of the devil, The Victim's one and only guard popped out the house, carryin' old fashioned wrapped presents in his arms, higher than his face, and behind him's a fat, bald-egghead with more presents, egghead in the gray-pinstriped-Brooks-Brothers-suit, the corporate armor with the wing-tip shoes. I'd seen his pic in the paper for his GOOD DEEDS but he looked fatter in 3-D. Oh he was testin' the seams of the suit. And I'd never seen a body-guard carryin' presents like that so I start to laughin' and Arturo starts to shout "Merry Christmas." Giant Body Guard Fuck peeked from behind the gifts and caught a load of us. He dumped the shit and went to draw. I hit him with the Tae Kwon Do. Spinnin' back kick to the solar-plexus. Like steppin' on a wedding cake. It released that buzzy chemiskull in me: the spin, the hit, the thud. There's a jingle right before Gene whacks 'im with the X-Mass Tonfa, busts his head like a piñata.

Humpty Dumpty shrieks, blows the wrapped boxes and waddles for the house. I let Gene and Arthur fight over the spilled candy, and make chase. Humpty's back's to me but I see him dip into his coat, do that gun-drawing hunch, and he whirls around at me with the pistola. I grab that hand in a wrist lock, pull him to one knee, then shove him toward the door. My ear lobes tinglin', my tongue's tinglin' too.

That squirmy bastard popped up and tried to slam the door in my face. I took a flyin' stomp and knocked it open and him over. Inside the air conditioned house, I kicked him in the ass and gave Humpty a chance to dumpty up the stairs. So he makes like he's fumblin' then turns and flips a punch at me. Really! I didn't have to block that fat-fingered-flabby-armed punch, but he was so game I had to teach him a lesson. I shoved my forearm in the way of his punch and he grunted.

"Blam, blam, blam!" I shouted that right then 'cause that

was when a regular thug would've blown holes in him, or a member of The Invisible Hand in good standin' would've had the storm troopers ready to retaliate. I kicked this guy in the ass again. And I felt more of that tinglin' in my head, that electricity in the tips of my fingers, the adrenaline in my throat. I gave Humpty enough distance to keep him within the grasp but also to let 'im run to the room he felt safest in.

The home was high-domed, the style of the time, with antiques all over. Victim must've been on his way to the party but something had held him back. How brilliant The Hand. Gettin' everyone else out the house, workin' months and months being friendly to Body Guard, who we could now call Body Bag, so that he would be a friendly Fuck, slow to draw, ready to die under gift wrap.

Victim passed a first door in the hall to get to . . . where else? The wide room with the main frame, the processor, and things I don't know what. Again, I stomped the door open. Now he was cornered.

"You punks don't know who you're fucking with," he tried to explain. "I got connections."

"They've been severed," I let him know.

There in the corner, he started cryin'. Singin' to me. Singin' a little love song, a baby lullaby to the beat of my big-boom-box-heart.

Behind me, I could hear my little elves knockin' shit over, shoutin' challenges to anyone I might have missed on the way in. "Aqui," I shouted. "Aca 'stoy. It smells in here. It smells like this Fuck shit his pants." They barged in, jolly.

We surrounded him, circled him slowly. We stopped, and Arturo gave him the decree: "Welcome to the Bad Boy Room." Victim was singin' louder, slowly circling in the middle of us, watchin' me, singin', with his eyes squinted, rubbin' his temple with his left hand, openin' and closin' his right. "I have money," he cried. "Fuck the International . . . no . . . The Invisible Hand, Fuck those murderers. I know all about them. Together we can beat them."

We circled, his shoes squeakin' as he squinted, rubbed, opened and closed. "You're next," he said. "They turned on me, and I'm one of 'em. If they came for me, it's only a matter of time before they come for you motherfuckers." He stopped sobbin'. Now he tried shoutin' along with the rubbin'. "You're just a bunch of Spics to them. They don't even call themselves this 'Invisible Hand' shit. They laugh at you when you call 'em that shit. They're really called The International Oligarchy. They call the Head of The Dog 'The Bitch.' You're their Bitch. They throw you a bone and laugh while you and the niggers and chinks fight over it."

I should've put 'im away right away, what with me workin' with such impressionable minds like Gene and Arthur, but I liked watchin' the man squirm, talk that shit that'd done him so much good—that had gotten him the joint he was about to die in—and had done him so much bad—he was about to die.

"You stupid sons-of-bitches. Did you really think it would be this easy? Did you really think you could just waltz in and kill a member of The Invisible Hand? You think you're so fucking smart. Didn't the ease of all of this shit make you suspicious? You stupid bitches. This was a test to see if you dared to bite The Hand that feeds."

One of our three minds was thinking about the bribe, one of our three minds was thinking about the trap, one of our three minds was thinking about The Bitch.

And the man kept rubbin' and rubbin' his temple like he thought a ray might shoot out or somethin'. He was doin' it so much it got me a little nervous, and I was glad when he looked at someone else.

"You lie, you old Fuck," Arthur told 'im. "I was sittin' at The Long Table in The Hall of Doom when Gene drew our assignment from The Leather Sack." He sounded like a kid describing The Boogey Man. He went on, "You know, a Yellow Head Fuck was holdin' the bag, and the card with our symbol read 'Busca La Paz De La Mano' and it had your zodiac all over it. And the other

Heads of The Dog were jealous." Boogey, boogey, boogey, I swear is what it sounded like to me, and I didn't want to hear that sound any more. I went with a hammer fist to the bridge of Victim's nose.

And he blocked it!

We were all equally suprised.

Victim then tried a wide right hook to somewhere on my head. Of course, that was too much. I grabbed the arm, locked it and flipped The Fuck.

"Did you think it would be that easy, Bitch," I yelled at him. "You can't fuck over La Mano."

And again he went with the sobbing. That Gene Fuck booted him in the yarbles. We heard the noise, that squishy noise and Victim's song was then pretty.

"No more of the old in out in out for you," I told him. Arthur jumped on Victim with both feet. By the shoulders I picked that Fuck up, heavy from the beatin'. That Gene Fuck took a runnin' start and kicked Victim Fuck's head in the mouth. The lips slumped where his teeth gave in. Gene Fuck kicked until the lips pried open and the teeth spilled out with a chunk of blood. It all spilled out on the white marble floor, red, red, red, with a thick stringy vein leadin' from Fuck's mouth to the snow floor. Him glakin', making that noise. My muscles gettin' tighter, windin' up for that last hit.

Arthur Fuck picked him up by the hair. Tufts came off, so it took a few pulls, and I cocked my arm and punched Victim in the throat. It got his eyes crossed, and he slipped to the ground.

I kept kickin' Victim Fuck's old head, waiting for bits and bytes to fly out, but all there was was veins and brains. There he was, Humpty Dumpty layin' sunny-side up in his ripped suit.

I shouted, "Harem," the decree for the pillage to begin.

Gene kicked the closest wall, left a black smudge on it, knocked over the closest computer, just wanted to break shit, maybe take something that'd remind him of this night, another night he broke shit. That Arthur Fuck was a little less destructive but only 'cause he was on the lookout for the easiest shit to carry, the easiest to sell, a few more bucks.

I stepped into the hallway and back into my normal heart rate. I stepped back into my breath as Gene and Arthur scampered through the abode. The last of my buzz was evaporatin' through my skin. But there was enough stuff swirlin' in me to think strange things. Like . . . like that somehow Victim was juiced-up. Otherwise, how in the Fuck did he block my hammer fist? I'm no fool, I've stole a book or two, so I knew oh so well that the finger does not always know what the hand is doing. There's scheme after scheme after scheme layered below and above what I'm carrying out.

Logically, Victim could've been scared so bad his reflexes were on hyperspeed. Or maybe, just maybe, and I thought this for only one weird second, maybe he had some kind of micro-chip in his head he was trying to activate but it didn't work. Some shit like that though, if he had it, and The Hand knew he had it, The Hand, by right, would have to let us know about some shit like that, or maybe they would want that themselves. Or maybe I needed heat to straighten me out.

At the top of the stairs was the little-tit control for the central air, and I killed it. Picked up the potted plant under it and hurled it through a huge window to let H-town in, its hot, steamin' tentacles, the underpasses, the overrun fields between the hypermarkets, the pawnshops, the titty bars, the cemetery, the nests of flying roaches in the palm trees.

With the steam hissin' through, I had to find something to turn this into a monument, as The Invisible Hand had ordered. Now I felt stupid calling them that, because of what Victim Fuck had said about us being The Bitch, about some International Oligarchy. But The Hand was the name I knew them by, and all I could handle thinking of them as at that moment. So, for the sake of my generous and dangerous sponsors, I had to look for the ritual they had ordered created. I had to look for a signature, some sign to leave to scare the Hell out of people, for a while. And if I did a good job, *we* would be let Off The Dog, I'd been told.

We Browns would be allowed to rise to the level that opens all levels once you are off The Dog.

The door at the beginning of the hall, the one Victim passed, was a picture room, with photos and books, with only one big light blue flowery covered chair, comfy. I sat in it.

Over the rolltop desk was a painting of the gentleman in the other room. A 2-D version of the man runnin' out of dimensions in the next room, each dimension slippin' away. I thought of shovin' the body in the desk. But that would be a Gene trick, horrify people the wrong way. Not exactly the touch called for.

I needed a second to wonder why The Hand picked Victim, why him? How'd he cross The Hand?

Was gettin' mixed up with The Hand the only way Victim could've gotten all these nice things?

I like to think me and everyone else on The Dog was just dealt a bad hand. What if no one could get ahead without them? What if we were all bitches?

I could tell from the pictures, which were gettin' cloudy now, covered with Octo-juice, Victim had everything most everyone else wanted, family, nice home. Amazin' to think of how The Invisible Hand touches everything, touched the button that let the light into the camera to take pictures in the room. Posed the people just right. Shuttered away. Made the gold-dipped frames around those frozen moments, made those frames more attractive than the imitation wood ones, the silver ones. Adjusted the frames at just the right angles, the family photo there in the middle of the little table, the kids' pics on each side, angled like wings in mid flap, like the family's picture had wings, and those wings were the pictures of the kids graduatin', all the kids at the park for some reason, and it's a sunny day. It doesn't seem hot at all in the pictures. Sometimes it's nice in Houston.

Yes, I would concoct something that would elevate Victim to the level of the *People's Martyr*. He would become the people's true false-prophet. The real prophets, we remain alone.

I could hear glass breakin', furniture gettin' tipped over, boots stompin' as it got warmer and warmer. Gene ran by carryin' a long full-length mirror through the hall. I knew he knew I was in here, saw me out of the corner of his eye but knew to leave me alone. Even though they acted stupid sometimes, Gene and Arthur knew there were three parts to every Head of the Dog and three parts to each of those Three Heads and each one was carefully formed by The Invisible Hand.

I slipped the picture of the family out of its frame and read the back. There was nothin' written on it. Eventually everyone in the picture would move on, die, the picture would get passed on, but without writing on the back, who would know who was who or where or why it was taken.

It's a shame. To not try to stick together at every moment at every turn, unless you've decided on the opposite path, only then turnin' away at every possible turn, every possible moment in order to get the message across, for the greater good, the ugly truth. I slipped the picture back into the frame, but I slipped it in upside down.

And later, that's what terrified everyone the most, the pictures upside down. Genio and Arturo were smokin' the house, shittin' on clothes, jaggin' off on plants, but all that simply made the public sick and appalled. Those two Heads just get you to cross to the other side of the street when I pass, to take a self-defense course, is random, somethin' that could happen to anyone.

What really scared everyone into a group, was me takin' out those pictures, family poses, shots of them familyin' around, me slippin' out those pictures and puttin' them back in upside down, placin' them carefully where the previous hand had set them. 'Twaz the act that scared *the public, the people* into a huddled mass, an angry huddled mass, a vigilant mask mad enough to kill their differences, melt prowlers' guns, spank the good boys, kiss the bad girls, spray the Korporate inc unto good books for bad kids, poor the feed.

My black clothes stuck to my skin. I found a fat, black marker in the desk and scratched and rescratched an "X" on the door, resketched and sketched, as the place got hot, as Gene and Arthur killed the air with their sweat, their hoots, hollers, crashes, bandido-isms. My other two heads would respect my mark and leave this room alone because I had invented what was needed to create the monument.

I stepped into the hall. The walls in the rest of the house were covered with paint, scrawls on the wall, lines, jagged lines, which no one tried to interpret after the fact, but my pictures left everyone guessin'. Was it a threat to everyone in the family? Did it mean they were next? Was it a pattern, a quirk? Did I know them? Was this revenge? Were all families at risk? Was I lashin' out at my own family? No one was safe. But not because of me. I was tryin' to save them.

The alarm started rattlin', lights flashin'. That Gene Fuck was still carryin' that mirror as he turned the corner and ran through the hall right past me, laughin' and laughin' and laughin'. That Arthur Fuck was right behind him, carryin' a bag of goodies. "That Gene Fuck hit the alarm," he shouted.

"On purpose?"

"On purpose."

I don't think there's much you can do about a Gene Fuck. Lucky for him, our jobs were done. I ran down the stairs.

"Holy shit," I could hear Gene, who made it out the door first. "Holy Shit." I stopped when I saw it too. There was water fillin' and splashin' and risin' and racin' up the steps, all around the house—a moat. A cool breeze rose from the spillin', a mist where the breeze fuckt the hot air, bubbles that hist smoke when they popped. I could make out large creatures movin' in it, their round heads, tentacles stickin' out. The water gurgling higher and higher, a *moat* around the fucking house.

"Jump. Drop your shit and jump." I ran to the highest stair showin', leapt to the top of the limo then jumped for the other side, landin' on my elbows and knees, my foot splashin' a little, getting nipped at by something in the water as the water crawled after me faster. I scrambled for higher ground and looked over my shoulder. There they were, runnin'. Gene with that mirror over his head like it might be a wing, jumping like he was tryin' to fly, sinkin' over the spot where the limo had been devoured by the water. Arthur tuckin' the bag into his side like it was a football, runnin' down the stairs right into the moat like he might plow through it. That's how they looked before they went under. One tentacle over the mouth, one around the throat, one around the arms. That's how we die. Underwater. Clutching what we prize most. A surpised look on our faces.

I always wonder if they hadn't gotten just a little tug from behind, just enough to keep them from makin' it over.

The Invisible Hand knew what Victim was like and helped shape him. The Hand knew what Gene was like and helped shape him. But that same Motherfuckn' Hand didn't feel like warning me about this little suprise moat.

You never know, really. All the ins you got, all the outs you can think of and you never really know. You never really know "why not me?"

There was nothin' for me to do but run. My heart was double-poundin' from the alarm, from the fall, from the makings of a trap. But I could not move.

The alarm came back into the focus of my hearing and was answered by sirens. The sirens taunted me, seduced me with beautiful songs of my exploits, called me hero, told me not to move, not to fear.

A cop ran to the edge of the dark water and shouted, "I can't cross."

I knew not to fear the cops. I could feel a halo around me, knew they could do nothing to me. But I didn't know if the halo had been put there by The Invisible Hand, by Chance, or by Fate. And I was scared because it's impossible to know if a gift from The Invisible Hand is a present, a bribe, or a threat.

I could hear but could not feel the heavy flap of the helicopters' wings sending ripples, shaking the water and the ground, blowin' away the last of the smoke, burstin' the last of the smoke-filled bubbles, fanning the sulphur smell. The helicopters circled Victim's house, their spotlights shinin' like little stars of Bethlehem descending upon me.

Rick Najera

Rick Najera has written for several television shows, including In Living *Color, The Robert Townsend Show, Culture Clash* and *The Paul Rodriguez Comedy Special.* He is currently the executive producer for Galavision's *Kiki Desde Hollywood.* In addition, he has co-written four television pilots for Universal Studios, Paramount Studios, HBO and UPN. He is the author of *The Pain of the Macho.*

Hollywood Heretic

I was once asked to speak to a large rally of Mexican Americans in Sacramento, a Cinco de Mayo Rally. I stood on the bandstand, five thousand Latinos looking at me. I felt exhilarated. I felt a surge of pride and excitement. The crowd was hushed.

I started my speech by saying how much I loved my people. I immediately knew I had struck a universal cord. I said that I was proud to be Latino. I avoided the dreaded "H" word—Hispanic—because it was a predominantly Chicano crowd.

I said I was proud to be Chicano even though I had very little to do with being Chicano. It was my parents and a margarita and a decision. (Actually, I might've picked British royalty if I could be guaranteed their money while keeping my Latin good looks.)

I said I was proud to be Chicano, proud of my *Raza*, my race, my "cosmic race." I knew I was a product of European and Indigenous blood, a mix, a *Mextizo*. I had been blended much like a margarita, over 30 years ago. (In Hollywood years, I was really twenty-one.)

I said to the now-frenzied crowd, "I love my *Raza*." I said it twice for the power of repetition, like a drumbeat. The crowd came to its feet. I said, "*¡Que viva la Raza!* Long live my *Raza!* Long live my race!"

The crowd was at a fever pitch. My voice amplified through the loud speaker, echoed past the rally into the heart of the capitol Sacramento, California, a rich state, rich with my people. And now in front of me stood thousands waiting for a call to action.

"¡QUE VIVA LA RAZA!" I cried.

Now, they were chanting with me. "¡QUE VIVA LA RAZA! ¡QUE VIVA LA RAZA!"

Out of the corner of my eye, I saw a scared Anglo family eating their barbecue. They weren't chanting. They sat with muted looks, their "Pollo Loco" lunch in front of them. They had come for the *folclorico* dancing, and they were probably the only ones in the rally that had. Already they had been invaded gastronomically, now I was invading their precious psyche, crossing the border of their minds. Deep would this memory live within them.

"¡QUE VIVA LA RAZA! I love my race—*La Raza*. The Race."

At the climax of my rant and shared chorus of fellow Chicanos, I screamed, "Do you know who else loved their race? The Nazis!"

The crowd stopped. It was like a photograph in front of me. *¿Que? ¿Que?* was their collective murmur. I thought of my mom, as most Latino men do at times of crisis or when we look at our mates and think, "Why can't you love me and adore my like my mother does? And why won't you cook me a good meal?" But that's another story.

"We need to be inclusive, not exclusive," I yelled.

As we become the majority, what lessons will we learn? What lessons will we teach? There are thirty million odd Latinos in the United States. And I am one of the oddest because I am an artist. I don't feel at home in my culture, and I don't feel at home in the Anglo culture. I don't feat at home. I was never meant to.

My work in life, if work is what defines us, is to speak the unspeakable, and that is why I am a heretic.

We need to be inclusive, not exclusive.

We must never repay prejudice or the worse form of racism—indifference—in kind. We must, somehow, be better than that. Better than who we know ourselves to be or can imagine that our *Raza* must be. Better than ourselves. Cultural pride must not be exclusive. We are an all-you-can-eat buffet, from *tostones* to *frijoles* to apple pie—just fry our apple pie in a flaky tortilla shell.

Cultural pride is a two-edged sword.

That's why I am a heretic in Hollywood.

I see that Hollywood or the culture of entertainment is *exclusive,* that our stories are not told. We are not heard.

Saving Private Ryan had no Latinos, yet Latinos are the most decorated of all groups, but obviously we are camera-shy when it comes to World War II and Korea.

Recent Screen Actors Guild surveys have pointed out the appalling misrepresentation of Latinos. We have been *excluded*.

And for that reason, my writing has been seen by some as heretical, at least in Hollywood. I have been a voice in the wilderness. Our story will be told.

I have sold TV pilots to all the major networks, yet none have reached the airwaves.

I have been given accolades and awards, yet there has never been a moment when I felt I belonged.

I currently have an office at Paramount Studios. "Currently" in Hollywood means "could be canceled at any moment." I produce a bilingual show. But English-speaking Latinos are nonexistent or invisible in this medium, this culture of Hollywood.

This culture of Hollywood is not Anglo, Jewish, or Black, or Asian, or Hispanic. It is Hollywood.

Hollywood is a culture unto itself, and once you become a member of this community, you must give up your culture and its baggage. Leave it at the guard gate of your studio. By the way, the guard will most likely be Latino.

And when you do bring your culture, Hollywood will decide which aspect of your culture it will focus on: gang banger, Latin Lover. They will decide your story, and it may not even be cast with a Latino in it. After all, Anthony Hopkins was Zorro. . . .

So what must we do?

Nothing.

Our mere existence is doing it.

We know the prize. We are not wanted, nor will we ever be. Unless you are willing to leave your culture at the gate.

No. The answer is work. Tell your story unabashedly, without apology. Be inclusive—offend Anglo, Latino, and Antarctican alike. Include them all in your world as you see it. Be a heretic. And smile secretly to yourself because you have a great ally at your side, and no one knows it.

Your ally is population growth.

By the middle of the next century, one in four Americans will be Latino. Your sheer numbers are on your side. You will win.

But here is the irony. The two worse things in life are wanting something badly but not getting it, and wanting something badly and getting it.

Buena suerte. Best of luck.

Manic Hispanic

"Sabotage" by the Beastie Boys plays. It's hard and driving music. He or she is an expensively dressed, light-skinned Latino/Latina. The Manic Hispanic is in his/her postmodern office. We see an expensive large desk and a big leather executive chair behind it. Manic Hispanic sits on his/her chair as the lights come up. The performer's back is to the audience.

MANIC HISPANIC: Nice view, great view, huh? You're wondering why God smiled on me. Maybe it's a quota system. Maybe I don't deserve it. I'm the universe expressing itself. I deserve wealth and happiness. I deserve an espresso. (*Manic Hispanic turns around.*)

Phil, bring me an espresso. Never hire Anglos—they won't work. I don't care about the prestige.

I have to remember that it's okay to love me.

I was so messed up before I went to therapy. I even went to a psychic. She told me I had three past lives. I said, "Stop the karma merry-go-round, I want to get off."

She said that I was an Egyptian eunuch in the twelfth century. That explains my fascination with castration.

Then she says I was a Chinese concubine in the thirteenth century. That explains my fascination with silk.

Then in 1940, I was a Mexican taxi driver who was beaten to death at a piñata party by a deaf eight-year-old. That explains my fascination with baseball, 'cause I'm not Dominican.

Wow, three past lives. Talk about bad luck: a minority in three past lives. God, why couldn't I be British royalty just once? Why do I get the boring past lives? Well, life's unfair. Some people are unlucky. But not me and not anymore. I got lucky. I got well and, now, it's my turn to make other Latinos lucky.

And right now, you got lucky. Life smiled on you because I loved your script *Cortez and Montezuma*. What a great film! Cortez and Montezuma, what wonderful characters. I see Jeremy Irons and Paul Rodriguez in the leading roles. You did make Cortez look like a bad guy. But we can lighten him up in the rewrites, especially if we get Robin Williams to play Cortez,to bring out Cortez's comedic side . . . or Jim Carrey. We can emphasize Cortez's discovery of this great culture and downplay the massive destruction of it.

This market is going to be huge.

I even adopted a little Latino kid to start. I have this problem with commitment. My roommate Enrique/Erica said I should do something nice, so I adopted this little Third-World Latino kid. There's his picture on the wall. He's the one with the flies on his forehead. I'm just worried that someday I'll get a knock at my door. I'll see some kid saying, "You remember me? I got one stinking letter and a few pennies a day. I'm Paco from Peru." *(She/He laughs when she/he realizes there's no response.)*

It feels good to help out a fellow Hispanic. I'm Hispanic. That's why the studio felt I would have a perspective on this project. I know what you're thinking. Am I Latino enough to get your project? Have I experienced the pain of my people? *(Beat.)*

Uh . . . no. But I'm full Mexican. I don't care what that nasty rumor says. I'm pure Mexican. I'm just light. My sister's dark; she's got a lot of Indian blood. I know that, 'cause when I was young, I used to have her build me Spanish missions in my backyard and I converted her to Catholicism. I stole her gold jewelry and gave her chicken pox. *(Beat.)*

That was a joke. You Chicanos can be so serious.

I went to a Chicano Studies Program. They thought I wasn't Chicano. "Oh, please, let me join your oppressed minority group." They thought I hadn't felt enough oppression. And I said, "Pepe, does right now count?"

I was on a plane once and a stewardess came up to me and said, "Are you an Hispanic?" I said, "Yes, but I'm not leaving first class." I thought it was going to be one of those Rosa Parks-back-of-the-bus moments. Then she said, "This man is having medical difficulties; we need you to translate using your best Spanish possible." So I walked up to the man and said *(heavy Spanish accent).* "Chew are going to die." I speak horrible Spanish. But I'm still Hispanic. *(Calms down.)*

Do you like that? I got that statue at Cancun. Great Mayan pyramids in Cancun. I went to Cancun in a Club Med weekend to get in touch with my indigenous roots with my roommate. She/He has full lips, strong muscles and is a beautiful tennis player. So I walked to the top of this newly discovered Mayan pyramid. I saw the mist of the jungle rise up as my people would have seen it thousands of years ago. *(Truly in awe and touched sincerely and simply.)*

I felt for once I belonged to something other than myself. I was truly touched. The confusion I sometimes feel vanished. I knew who I was, where I was from, where I was going. I was in the middle of it all, where it began, and I knew peace. *(Confessional.)*

I'm very light and tall. My family must have been from the northern area of the Yucatan, near the Alps. So, I'm on top of this Mayan pyramid and I see this little Indian head hidden in the rocks. I was touched. No one had seen this little sculpture for over a thousand years, and I was in awe.

My Mayan side was in awe, but my Spanish conquistador side thought it would've made a neat bookend. So I broke it off and brought it here and made it into an ashtray. *(The spell is gone and the Manic Hispanic is back.)*

You can put your cigarette butts right there, in the Indian's head. All right, we've bonded. *(Angrily, with menace.)*

Now, about your script: let's make Cortez look like the good guy.

BLACKOUT

Lionel G. Garcia

Lionel G. Garcia's books include *I Can Hear the Cowbells* and *A Shroud in the Family*. He has received awards from PEN Southwest and the Texas Institute of Letters, among others.

The Apparition

Father Procopio jiggled his eyebrows once more, a sure sign that he had changed images in his mind, gone from the infamous brown and white apparition that he had been seeing every morning for the last week against the church wall, gone to the many-colored picture of his mother coming at him with his father's belt, her hand raised in passion, ready to strike him anywhere on the head. Father Procopio, aware that his mother was about to hit him, jumped from his bed in the morning heat, feeling his stupor melting, and fell on his knees on the floor next to his wrinkled shoes. He reached over and gathered his pants from the chair next to his bed and brought along with his pants the frayed white shirt that rested on top. In the solitude of the darkness of his room he instinctively took out from his pants pocket his miniature rosary and began to pray as he stayed on his knees and attempted with difficulty to put his clothes on before the nosy Pimena entered the room with his coffee. He looked at the clock on the dresser and saw five o'clock in the morning. The old rooster had not yet crowed. The mosquito that had bothered him all night long rested, his rear-end upright, next to his pillow. He took the rosary and swatted at it in anger, and it flew away unharmed, disappearing from his focus right in front of his very eyes. He followed the sound as the mosquito droned his way up toward the rafters of his room to hide for the day. Father Procopio felt on his body where the insect had taken enough of his blood during the night to last for a week. Outside the door he could hear the housekeeper, Pimena, picking up the tufts of hair that the cats had deposited in the hallway during the day. He could smell the cup of coffee in her hand.

"Cats, cats, cats," he could hear her complain as she swept cat hair from the floor of the hallway with her hand. "First it was collecting bottles and then cats and then collecting fleas from the cats and putting them in bottles and now we are into bed-bugs and putting the bedbugs in little tin boxes. When he doesn't collect one thing, he collects another. He reminds me of the raccoon. The next thing we know he'll be washing his food at the table before he eats it. It's a good thing the Bishop is coming to see about the apparition. When the Bishop sees the rectory, he's going to make the good Father consent to clean it up. And I need extra help. The Bishop will see that. I've been working on cleaning the attic for the last two weeks. A lot of good it does to clean only the attic. There were more bottles and bottles with fleas and little tin boxes with bed-bugs and cat hairs than any human would believe."

Having heard her, Father Procopio crossed himself twice with the small bronze crucifix and said a minuscule prayer for Pimena, a prayer to make her mind her own business. Before Pimena could knock, Father Procopio gauged the motion of her actions, imagining through the wooden door as the elderly lady raised her hand to knock. "Enter, by all means," he said as Pimena held her hand in check.

"This man knows everything," she said, filled with mystery, as she opened the door, walking stooped from having had to clean the house of the cats' hairs for three years.

"How are you this morning, Pimena?" the good Priest asked her.

"Fine, Father," Pimena responded. "How long have you been praying?"

"Just now," Father Procopio said, adjusting the sleeves of his long shirt. "I have just now started."

"By the time you finish, the coffee will be just right," Pimena said, wiping the tabletop of cat hairs and placing the coffee next to the clock. "And don't forget to say a little prayer for me. And for my back and for all the work I had to do in the attic."

"I already did," Father Procopio told her. He moved his weight from one knee to the other, rocking from one side to the other. "I think that I'm getting too old to do this anymore," he informed Pimena. "Maybe God will forgive me if I pray sitting down."

"You know very well the Bishop has written that it takes ten prayers sitting down to equal one kneeling down," Pimena reminded him.

Of course he knew, goddammit, irritated that the ignorant Pimena presumed to remember better than he. Had it not been he that had read the Bishop's letter to the congregation, the ten-page letter that explained in detail how one should pray, not only the prayer itself, but how one must chose the proper stance, the proper lighting to aid in the comfort of the task? "The light must fall over the left shoulder," the Bishop had written. His mind was suddenly distracted at how irritatingly ignorant the Bishop was. These people were doing good to come to church and sit down, much less be preoccupied with the light coming over the left shoulder. "If one knows how to read, the holy book should be at least eighteen inches from the front of the eyes. Any shorter distance will tire out the vision. One must remember that the idea behind prayer is that one must be comfortable not only with the written word but in God's presence. However, too much comfort can impede prayer. Here I am referring to the practice that some people have of praying sitting down. This is well and good and our Father recognizes such prayers. However, it is my contention that prayers recited while kneeling are found more receptive by our Father. If someone would ask me for exact figures I would be hard pressed to answer, but taking a wild guess I would venture to say that our Father considers a prayer offered kneeling down to be ten times more effective than one sitting down."

"How is it outside?" he asked, nervously skipping over from the first to the last mystery of his tedious rosary.

"There are only a few out there," Pimena answered as she went to look out the window at the churchyard below. "The true believers. But it's very early. Wait and see at eight o'clock when the sun has been out a few hours."

"Of all churches . . . that it would have to happen to this one. The one with the most lunatics," he said as he sat on the bed to put on his shoes.

"The Ladies of the Altar Society will begin selling snow cones today. I saw Olivia and Sixta trying to buy ice yesterday," Pimena told him.

Father Procopio jiggled his eyebrows and changed mental gears. He was now seeing the Altar Society reserving ice for today, the large Olivia, her gold medallion swinging from breast to breast as she lead the group of four women through the dusty streets of San Diego. Not only were they looking for ice, they were in search of volunteers, someone to patrol the churchyard now that the Mother Superior and her three nuns had gone on vacation for the summer.

"If only the Mother Superior was here," Pimena lamented, knowing well that she was irritating the Priest and that all his morning prayers would be canceled on their way to Heaven by Father Procopio's anger.

"Don't even say that," Father Procopio replied as he stood up, gritting his teeth. He jammed his rosary into his pants pocket. It would be blasphemous to continue praying.

"And your rosary?" Pimena asked as she picked cat hairs from her arms.

"I'll just have to pray it later on," the harried Priest informed her.

"You'd better do it before sun up because you know how many people will be in the courtyard today. Word of the apparition has reached all of south Texas. Everyday more and more come."

Father Procopio adjusted his suspenders over his shoulders and took a sip of coffee. "I know," he murmured to himself.

"Father?"

"Yes, Pimena."

"Well, I don't know whether to ask you or not. Maybe you've already thought about it and have rejected the idea."

"What are you talking about?"

"Some of the people in my poor neighborhood have been asking me to ask you. But it's up to you and the Mutualists. Whatever you say goes. You know that, don't you, good Father?"

Father Procopio looked at her with much hate. She had ruined his rosary. He was tired of hearing her complain about his cats. She was not keeping the rectory clean. It was not he, it was she, Pimena, that was dirty. Twenty cats was not too much for one household, not one where there was almost nothing to do except to move dust around.

Father Procopio whistled softly and this time the noise of nineteen cats was heard as they ran down the stairs in anticipation of the morning's blessing and the milk that he would give them. Only the faithful Princess, his most favorite cat, the one that had come to him one night as he walked and prayed for his soul, stayed behind. Father Procopio realized what a prize she was. Any cat that would prefer him to milk and blessings in the morning had to be special. Princess walked into Father Procopio's room very deliberately, seductively, her back arched, and went over to the legs of the dresser and rubbed her body around the them. She meowed twice and went over to Father Procopio to be stroked and kissed on the top of the head.

"Now what were you saying, Pimena?" Father Procopio asked her as he continued to stroke and love Princess.

"I was just talking, good Father," Pimena replied, embarrassed as usual at seeing Father Procopio show so much love to an animal.

"What were you going to ask?" Father Procopio wanted to know as he stroked his beloved cat.

"I was saying about you and the Mutualists. And how whatever you say goes."

"I know that what I say goes, Pimena. I wish to God that you would understand that I know that. I know everything, Pimena. As far as you are concerned, I know everything."

"That is exactly what I tell everyone in town, good Father. That you know everything. You even know when I'm about to knock on the door, as though you could see through wood."

Father Procopio put the cat down and finished his coffee in one large swallow. He smacked his lips, felt Princess's cat hair sliding down his throat and said, "I can see through wood. And I know how to anticipate. I know everything that is going on about me."

"And the apparition? How do you explain that, Father Procopio?" Pimena teased the good Father.

Father Procopio buttoned the top of his shirt and made a grunting sound as though he was thinking about picking up something with which to hit the woman. Princess ran out of the room when she heard the unfamiliar grunt. Pimena stepped back indecisively, but with much respect. She knew how frustrated he was in trying to explain the apparition. Instead of venting his anger on her he lit a cigarette and pointed the match at her. "I tell you Pimena that that is the only thing that has ever baffled me in my life."

"It is religion," Pimena said innocently, surprised that the Father had not at the very least burned her with his cigarette as he did the Altar Boys. "Only God knows those things. I myself thank God for making me ignorant, if you must know. I wouldn't know what to do if I was in the Altar Society. So much knowledge. It would break my head."

"Not necessarily," Father Procopio corrected her. "There really isn't that much knowledge to go around," he said.

"But religion," Pimena worried, "look at all that there is to it. Look at this apparition of our Blessed Mother that has taken over the wall of the church. How do we account for that?"

"I'll find out," Father Procopio informed her. "Religion is more of a science than you ignorant people think," he said.

"I've always said to the neighborhood and everyone that will listen that you know everything, Father Procopio."

"Oh, that it were true," the good Priest had to admit now that he was in control of his frustrations and at the present forgiving Pimena for destroying his morning prayer. Pimena scraped cat hair from her tongue and cleaned her wet finger on her apron. "And the people that ask me about the Wheel of Fortune . . . well, I say to them: 'Let the good Father worry about that. Maybe he's thought of that already and has dismissed the idea.' ' It would make money,' some say. 'Now's the time to drag it out. There are many people making a pilgrimage to San Diego. What harm would it do?' 'No,' I say to them. 'Father Procopio in his own time will decided if the wheel should come out. Andres Garcia is dead,' they say. They say there is no opposition to the Wheel of Fortune."

Father Procopio had not listened to Pimena. He had been lost in his thoughts about the apparition. Pimena took the empty cup and saw the cat hairs that stuck to the bottom and shook her head. "The cats will be the ruination of this house one day," she said.

Father Procopio took a huge drag from his cigarette and blew smoke at Pimena. "Just leave the cats alone," he said. "They are my life. I could not live without them and you know that."

"Well, Father, that was what you said about the bottles and now look at where they're at . . . hidden in the attic behind the boxes. Abandoned and dusty with no one to look over them. You haven't been to see them in over a year."

The Priest took in what he felt was the disgusting sight and smell of the old lady. "I tuck my cats to sleep every night. I go into the attic," he scolded her.

"But good Father, you never go to where the bottles are anymore," Pimena responded as she took the cup and tried to sweep cat hair from the table top. "You don't move them around or look at them like you did when you first started."

"I don't have to if I don't want to. The bottles are mine. Leave them alone. I don't want anyone touching them."

"Have no fear, Father. I didn't touch any of your precious bottles."

"Good," Father Procopio said, "I don't want anyone touching them except me."

"And the fleas and the bed-bugs, good Father?" Pimena asked him.

"The fleas and the bedbugs are mine also. I have a reason for saving them."

* * *

"Whatever you say, good Father," Pimena agreed with him. "Like I always say, 'Father Procopio is a lot smarter than he looks.'"

Father Procopio looked through the rafters, past the mosquito, to the heavens and whispered, "Dear God what have I done to deserve this: the Bishop, Pimena, San Diego and now the apparition. I wonder if the Baptists need a Catholic priest?"

"What did you say?" Pimena asked.

"Nothing," Father Procopio answered her brusquely.

"I thought I heard you speak."

"You need to clean your ears, Pimena."

"Yes, good Father. Like I cleaned the attic for the cats and the Bishop's beast."

"Yes," Father Procopio said bitterly, "the Bishop's beast. Did you make a bed for him?"

"Yes, good Father," Pimena said hurriedly, "I cleaned up real good right where he's going to sleep. I arranged a feather pillow for him just as you asked."

"Not as I asked," Father Procopio reminded her, "as the Bishop demanded."

"And the cats, good Father?" Pimena worried. "Will they do fine sleeping with the beast?"

The Priest looked out the window at the faint outline that was beginning to take shape on the church wall. He said, "The cats will do fine. They've done it before . . . slept with the beast, I mean. And besides, the attic is their home. I'm not going to move them just because of the Bishop's beast. And that is that. Bishop or no Bishop."

"I understand, good Father. But don't be so angry just because the Bishop is coming."

"It's not the Bishop. You make me angry. You think you'd know by now that the cats are not to be moved for any reason at all. And especially not for the Bishop's beast."

Pimena looked at the Priest with some distress. She said, "You never know, good Father. I just wondered if the cats and the horrible beast would get along; it's been so long."

"I'll worry about that, Pimena," said the Priest. "You're beginning to make me angry, so you'd better leave."

Pimena started to bow and walk backwards toward the door when she said, "Don't get so upset about the Bishop. You shouldn't hate him so much. Please don't argue with the Bishop. We would like to keep you as our Priest. You know how violent the Bishop can become."

"Just leave me alone, Pimena. Please," he pleaded. "Just leave me alone with my cats."

"Here," Pimena said, "I almost forgot." She had reached into her apron and pulled out a small glass jar. Father Procopio knew instantly what it was. "This came for you this morning from the crazy Bernabe."

Father Procopio's eyes danced as he counted the tiny bed-bugs inside the jar. "Fifteen," he whispered.

"That's all he could find last night he said," Pimena explained.

Father Procopio sighed and said, "Well, along with the other ones that I have in the attic that ought to be enough."

"It's a mystery to me but whatever you say, good Father," Pimena told him. She picked cat hairs from the sleeves of her blouse and held them at the tips of her fingers before shaking them to the floor. "But Father, look at this. The whole house is covered with cat hairs. It will ruin our health some day. It can't be normal to live with twenty cats."

Father Procopio puffed on his cigarette and flipped the ashes on the table. He grunted again in anticipation of his thoughts, scaring Pimena. "Just leave my cats alone," he said with so much conviction that Pimena backed out of the room using the empty cup of coffee as a shield. And as she did so she stepped on Princess, who had been waiting for Father Procopio in the hallway by the door.

"Watch what you're doing!" the good Father shouted at the old woman as she ran down the hallway, flew down the stairway to the first floor and cried her way into the kitchen.

She screamed from the kitchen as she ran, scattering the other cats waiting for their milk: "Forgive me Father. I didn't mean to step on your precious cat."

"It is Princess that has to forgive you," Father Procopio yelled down at her from the top of the stairs. "Look at the poor cat. Afraid of being hurt again. Ready to go hide in the attic. Come Princess, my beauty, we must have our morning's blessing and our milk. Pimena is mean, don't you think? I won't let her touch you again. I promise."

Pimena was right. By eight in the morning when the sun had cleared the tops of the salt cedars that surrounded the rectory, the apparition was perfectly formed on the church wall, and with the apparition came the people, some with large medallions in the shape of body parts, others with the less expensive body parts made of small tin pieces, others with photographs of loved ones in need of medical help or long ago dead. Some came from the front gate of the rectory on their knees to touch the wall.

Father Procopio looked out through the window of his small downstairs office at the crowd, at the abhorrent spectacle, and crossed himself. He thought for a moment and then looked at his watch. He got out of his office and went into the kitchen and looked for Pimena, and then through the window he saw her standing outside talking to Carmen, the youngest of the Ladies of the Altar Society. Pimena was crunching on a yellow snow cone which meant to Father Procopio that she had been recruited by the Ladies of the Altar Society as a volunteer to keep order on the church grounds.

He hurried up the stairs and the cats ran with him. He flung open the attic door and there on the floor by the window was the feather pillow that Pimena had fluffed for the Bishop's beast. Trembling, he opened four jars of fleas and poured the little insects into the pillow as the cats, licking themselves, watched in fascination. He took four tin boxes full of bedbugs

140

plus the glass jar that Pimena had given him and ran out of the attic to the room across the hall where the Bishop was to stay. Quickly, he threw off the sheets and scattered the starved bedbugs on the mattress.

He went back to his office, looked out to see Pimena still munching on her yellow snow cone, leaning against the icebox and probably telling everyone how smart Father Procopio really was. He put on his coat and walked out the rear door in order not to be seen. Still a few old ladies saw him and stopped him to bless their rosaries and the images of body parts. He waved his hand over the icons that they dangled in front of him, whispering the sign of the cross in Latin as the ladies offered him money, money that he turned down.

From the rear gate he could see Pimena now helping the four women of the Altar Society as they erected their tent under which they would sell their snow cones. He tried not to look at them to see if by God's good grace they would not see him. He opened the gate hurriedly, walked out into the street and closed the gate behind him. As he did so he turned up the street to walk to the depot and saw the Fat Amandito, Don Andres Garcia's dog walking next to him. Amandito, upon seeing the Priest, ran over to the fence that Father Procopio was crowding. As Amandito approached him, Father Procopio said, "I don't have time to talk this morning. I'm on my way to meet the train and the Bishop."

"Heaven help us then," Amandito prayed as he made the sign of the cross and then kissed his thumb. "I just now got through telling my dog that this would not be a good day for you, Father Procopio."

"That's presumptuous of you, Amandito, don't you think?" the Priest scolded him as he hurried on his way.

"Whatever that means, good Father," Amandito replied.

"Presumptuous, Amandito. To think that you know what will happen to me. I didn't know you could tell fortunes? The next thing we know you'll be joining the Ladies of the Altar Society and start explaining Catholicism to the old ladies."

* * *

Amandito kept up with the Priest stride for stride. "All I know is what I feel," he informed the Priest.

"Just be quiet," Father Procopio suggested. "Don't say a word. You're starting to irritate me."

Amandito, ignoring the Priest, let out a sigh as his inherited dog cut out in front of him. "This dog will be the death of me," he said, changing the conversation. "You just watch, good Father, one day they will find me dead in the street. I will have tripped over the dog and hit my head on a rock and killed myself."

"I don't have time to talk about your dog. I've already told you that I'm on my way to meet the Bishop."

"That must be hard on you, Father Procopio, as much as you hate the man."

"I don't hate the man, Amandito. Where did you get the idea?" he asked, thinking of the bedbugs.

"Oh, there is the talk about town. You know how everyone knows everything. And I myself can tell you hold no love for the man."

"We don't agree on some aspects of religion, if that's what you mean," Father Procopio informed Amandito. Feeling guilty, he quickened his pace to see if Amandito would stay behind.

"If you don't mind, good Father, I'll accompany you as far as the barber shop."

"Suit yourself, Amandito," Father Procopio said as he wiped the hair of twenty cats from his coat. "After all this is a public street.

"It must be hard on you not to agree with the Bishop on religion," Amandito kept on.

"It's none of your business, Amandito," Father Procopio let him know. "Whenever you start going to church then you can make it your business."

"Anyway, it's not good for the Bishop and the Priest not to agree on religion," Amandito told the Priest as the dog bounced in front of him and almost tripped him again. "Goddamn dog," he muttered so that the Priest was sure to hear.

"Don't curse in front of me, Amandito," Father Procopio warned him.

"I'm sorry, Father," Amandito remorsed, "but this dog will be the death of me."

Father Procopio studied the dog's rear and said, "You haven't castrated him like Don Andres asked you on his death bed."

"How could I?" Amandito pleaded. "You know that the doctor won't allow the dog in his office."

The dog weaved his way between Father Procopio's legs and made the Priest stumble. "See what I mean, good Father?" Amandito said. "The dog is constantly between one's legs or in front of one or behind one. He's always in the way. Always in some mischief. Just like the poor late Don Andres."

"You could take him to the veterinarian in Alice," Father Procopio said, jumping over the dog.

"But that would cost more than the doctor," Amandito informed him.

"Well, suit yourself," Father Procopio said. "I just don't like him hanging around my doorstep."

"I knew it!" Amandito cried. "I knew he was over at your house when he disappears."

"Just don't let him bother my cats," the Priest threatened him.

"I won't, Father," Amandito promised, feeling guilty for owning the dog.

The dog weaved his way around Amandito's legs and then came from behind and smelled Amandito's rear-end and then started to sneeze and couldn't stop, embarrassing Amandito. The Priest had seen what the dog had done but was content to ignore the indelicacy, hoping that ignoring the dog would spare him the act that the dog had performed on Amandito. But the dog was smarter than to be ignored and he knew instinctively that the ultimate embarrassment was to embarrass a Priest. So he quit sneezing and went over to the Priest and, almost tripping him, smelled his crotch and acted as though he were gagging.

Amandito adjusted his pants and retucked his shirt all around his waist as the dog went over to the fence and spit up a white froth. "What about the apparition, good Father? What is the meaning of such an important event? And in San Diego no less."

"I don't know," the good Father replied, trying to ignore what the dog was doing.

"Is it a good sign or a bad sign to have an apparition?"

"It depends on how it came about."

"Like what do you mean?"

"Well, is it a true apparition or is it false?"

"What if it's false?"

"Then we must expose it for what it is," Father Procopio said. "Contrary to what you ignorant people believe, religion is based on the truth. And the truth never hurt anyone."

"What will happen then if the people find out the truth?"

"Nothing. They'll accept it for what it is."

"Is this where you and the Bishop do not agree, Father?" Amandito asked as his dog came running to get in front of him.

"I suppose so, Amandito," Father Procopio said, jiggling his eyebrows and ducking out of the way as once more his mother swung the leather belt at his head.

Amandito stepped on the dog's foot and the dog gave out a shrill but short yelp. Despite the pain that made him limp, the dog refused to give ground, continuing to swing back and forth on three legs in front of the two men.

"Your dog, Amandito," Father Procopio concluded, admonishing the owner rather than the beast, "is very obtrusive."

"I'm sure you're right, good Father," Amandito agreed, looking down at the many-colored dog. "Whatever the word means."

Amandito and his limping dog stayed at the barber shop where the pair was greeted by the ne'er-do-wells that inhabited the town in great numbers. Father Procopio heard the screams run out of the small building as the men greeted Amandito and his dog. One of the men, who had never worked a day in his life, came out and shouted at Father Procopio that the train had not come in. Father Procopio, not knowing whether the drunk was lying or not, ignored the drunkard and kept on, not wanting to be made a fool.

As the Priest continued to the depot in the early heat of the day, he felt the morning sun against his black frock. He felt of the hot frock and without realizing it, he brushed away at the cat hairs on his sleeves as he wondered if he had used enough bed-bugs on the Bishop's bed.

On his way he could not remember whether he had heard the train whistle or not. When he arrived at the depot he found Don Tomas sitting quietly by himself on the bench, his wife having brought him over early in the morning so that he could talk to any passenger that might have the misfortune to have to wait for the train.

The drunkard at the barber shop had been right. The train had not arrived. If it had, the Bishop would have been there hugging his yapping beast and Don Tomas would surely have gotten hold of him by now. He cursed to himself so that God would not hear him, cursed that he had to find out for himself because the drunkards in this town were not to be trusted. In any other town, he assured himself, he would have turned back at the barber shop and saved himself the trip.

Just for that he would not take out the Wheel of Fortune.

He knew better than to let Don Tomas get started in conversation. He turned and ran out of the depot as soon as he saw the man, not giving Don Tomas a chance to get started on the diatribes on snakes breeding like dogs and possums fornicating through the nose and coyotes defecating on their offspring and the pee of the spider. He had heard all of this dirty talk before when he had had to kick Don Tomas out of the Mutualists. He couldn't take Don Tomas anymore than he could take the apparition, Amandito's dog, the Bishop, the Bishop's beast, Pimena,

Amandito, Bernabe, Fecundo, Faustino, and the Ladies of the Altar Society and their large gold medallions.

Father Procopio heard a slight sound, like a "Hey, Father" from Don Tomas as he ran away from the depot. He returned to the rectory taking a different route, not by way of the barber shop where the drunkards would laugh at him, but by way of the park and the kiosk where Andres Garcia had been flogged.

From the park across the street he could see the mass of people already invading the churchyard. He could hear the Ladies of the Altar Society lining up the people that wanted to buy snow cones. Pimena was at the front gate letting people in one by one, crunching the ice of a red snow cone. He crossed the street and went around the church, through the rear, around the parochial hall where he kept the Wheel of Fortune, and from there ran to the rear door of the rectory. Fortunately for him no one saw him except for Amandito's dog, who had mysteriously beat him back to the rectory and was lying at the doorstep.

From the upstairs window he could see the image he had been observing for the past mornings: a very slight resemblance of the Virgin Mary projected on the wall during the early morning hours, when the sun cleared the tops of the salt cedars that surrounded the rectory. One had to catch it before eleven o'clock at the latest. By that hour it would have moved and faded and disappeared.

Faustino, the drunkard, and Bernabe, the crazy one, had discovered it as they weaved their way home one morning. They had shown it to Pimena as she watered the salt cedars. To show it to Pimena had been the equivalent of showing it to the world. By the end of that day everyone in town knew about it. By the second day the surrounding communities knew about it. By the third day the newspapers from Alice and Corpus Christi knew about it and had sent reporters. By the fourth day the Bishop, sitting in the Bishopric in Corpus Christi having breakfast, had read the Corpus Christi newspaper. An hour later he had sent a telegram to Father Procopio inviting himself over to see for himself what the apparition looked like since the paper's photograph did not show anything and had to be doctored in order for the reader to see what the photographer had seen. And naturally, the Bishop and his beloved beast expected to stay with Father Procopio for a few days.

Father Procopio heard the train whistle as he jiggled his eyebrows and studied the figure intently. It fascinated him to see the downward movement that accompanied the apparition. Gradually he could see it work its way down so that by his watch, at eleven o'clock when the sun was almost overhead, the figure would disappear into the church ground and the faithful people would leave. The jiggling of his eyebrows turned his thoughts to his abandoned bottles and without bothering the lounging Princess and the other nineteen cats he went into the attic and worked his way through the twenty cat-boxes, the cat hair, and the feather pillow full of fleas that he had prepared for the Bishop's beast. He stepped over cartons of files—death certificates, birth certificates, church documents, marriage licenses—all from years and years ago. Not being able to climb over the wall of boxes, he began to move some of them out of his way in order to clear a path to the bottles.

Opening the path was a revelation. Pimena had lied. She had cleaned the bottles and had rearranged them differently, stacking most of them on the floor in rows of fours and fives, lining some of them on the window sill. Father Procopio cursed under his breath, raked cat hair from his tongue with his fingers and wiped the fingers on his thigh. He noticed the beam of light cutting across the room and looked to his left at the source. The sunlight, broad-beamed, was coming into the room through the window, crossing through the row of bottles, emerging as a converted thin beam across the room into the row of bottles on the opposite window, the one on the Priest's right. Cautiously, Father Procopio approached the beam of light. Without touching it or disturbing it in any way he studied the intensely bright beam as it crossed in front of him from the left window to the right.

He ducked under the beam and studied it from the opposite side and then he jiggled his eyebrows twice. Very carefully he went over to the right window and studied where the focused beam was entering one of the old hair-oil bottles that he had collected from the trash at the barber shop. After coursing through the glass, the beam was then directed downward and out over the church-yard and, like a lover sitting in the balcony of a cheap theater, he could see the white hot fan of light piercing the air to create the projected image on the movie screen—the church wall.

In order to satisfy himself, Father Procopio very gently placed the fingers of his right hand over the top of the hair-oil bottle and without disturbing the path of the beam he rotated the bottle ever so slightly as he watched the image below. Immediately he heard the roar from the crowd.

The effects had been unpredictable. The rotation of the apparition was something that no one had seen before. People began to faint and mass hysteria took over. The crowd, urged on by the Ladies of the Altar Society and the few old Mutualists that could leave home on their own, began to back away from the moving apparition. Father Procopio, looking down and smiling, slowly turned the bottle in the opposite direction and everyone began to scream and run.

The Ladies of the Altar Society were shoving the crowd away, yelling for everyone to leave the churchyard before the church exploded. Their tent and the icebox with the shaved ice and the snow cone syrup was knocked down by the running crowd. The wrought-iron fence that Father Procopio loved, the one that had been brought over from the cemetery, was torn down by the weight of the people that were trying to scale it. Pimena, who had been standing by the gate eating another snow cone had been the first to run and could be seen ahead of the pack running to-ward the center of town.

In a matter of seconds Father Procopio had cleared the churchyard except for the old intact dog that Don Andres Garcia, on his death bed, had given Amandito.

Just for spite, Father Procopio turned the bottle slowly and then rapidly back and forth and made the image disappear and reappear on the church wall as the growling dog watched the visual spectacle with unusual interest.

Across from where he stood, through the front window of the attic, Father Procopio could see a man dressed in white walking in a crouched, intimidated way, carrying a suitcase, hugging tightly against his chest his beloved beast, the ugly pug named La Poochie. It was the Bishop walking toward the church, wondering what all the commotion was about and what this congregation of humanity was doing running toward him. Father Procopio could see the Bishop tighten his hold on his dog as if to protect her, as if anyone would bother to steal a dog so ugly that she looked as though she had been sired by the Bishop himself. Nonetheless, La Poochie, not knowing that she was ugly, braced herself for the crowd that ran toward her and her master. As her heart quickened, she closed her eyes and prayed, expecting the worst. She felt the Bishop tighten his grip on her and she could hardly breathe through her short fat black nose. Then she felt the heaviness of his stride, her large head bobbing and weaving painfully, as the Bishop began to run. The crowd was screaming words that made no sense to her. When she finally opened her eyes, the Bishop had stopped running and she recognized the front of the rectory, except that now the gate and the wrought iron fence had been torn down by some mysterious force. Out of the corner of her large globular right eye she saw Amandito's dog as it growled and moved its head first to one side and then to the other, as Father Procopio played with the apparition on the wall. Instantly she recognized that this dog would cause her trouble during her stay, a stay that she had not wanted considering the condition of the rectory every time she visited, knowing that she had to endure not only the twenty cats and their hair but the pillow full of fleas. (Oh yes, she knew that Father Procopio hated her as he did the Bishop and added fleas to her pillow and bedbugs to the Bishop's bed, but she had no way of relaying the information to the Bishop.)

By the time the Bishop reached the door, Father Procopio was there to open it.

"Where is Pimena?" the Bishop asked as he took La Poochie from inside his coat and placed her on the floor.

"You didn't see her?" Father Procopio asked the Bishop. "She was at the head of the crowd that greeted you."

"What was that all about?" the Bishop wanted to know. "Did it have to do with the apparition?"

"Yes," smiled the satisfied Father Procopio. "It had all to do with the apparition."

"Then you must tell me, Father. I am very excited about this apparition if you must know. It is the talk of all south Texas. On the train all I could hear were the people talking about it. The train was full, by the way."

"It's been full for the last days. People are coming from all over, Your Excellency," Father Procopio said. Then looking at the Bishop's dog he said, "But not for long. This thing is about to end."

"Hogwash," the Bishop informed him. "You're always having a defeatist attitude, Father Procopio. Look at this as a gold mine . . . and heaven-sent too. Remember that everything that happens is the Lord's will. Take it. Take the opportunity that the good Lord gives you, Father. I would think that the episode of the Wheel of Fortune would have cured you by now."

"Don't you think you ought to take La Poochie out to do her business?" Father Procopio asked the Bishop as the poor dog panted her desire to go relieve herself.

"You're so right, Procopio," the Bishop said, picking up La Poochie and taking her outside.

"Remember, Procopio," the Bishop spoke as he and Father Procopio watched as La Poochie tried to relieve herself in the churchyard, "that this is a golden opportunity for your church and our diocese."

"I'm afraid I don't agree," Father Procopio replied.

"What do you mean, you don't agree?" the Bishop demanded to know.

"I don't agree at all. Wait until you see what I've discovered, Your Excellency."

"What do you mean?"

"Your trip may have been for nothing. I have solved the mystery of the apparition."

"The mystery, Father?"

"Yes, Your Excellency."

"I don't want to know about it. I don't want to know. Father Procopio, keep the information to yourself."

"Your Excellency, I can't. I have to show you."

"Father, I'm ordering you not to force me to look."

"I'll force you if I have to," Father Procopio informed the Bishop as the Bishop watched his beloved beast relieve itself of all that she had accumulated during the train ride.

"May I remind you, Father, that you are talking to your Bishop?"

"I don't mean to be disrespectful, Your Excellency."

"I wonder Procopio," the Bishop said, stroking his chin. "I wonder. There are rumors, you know."

"I know, Your Excellency," Father Procopio admitted.

"You know what I'm referring to, good Father?"

"Yes," Procopio replied.

"The other Priests have told me and it hurts me, Procopio."

"I know the other Priests have told you, Your Excellency."

The Bishop strolled around the churchyard taking in the disarray left behind by the large crowd. He shook his head. "We could make a fortune in snow cones, icons, little tin legs and arms, miniature automobiles, farm animals, tacos, lemonade, photographs. If only there were instant photographs," he murmured the recitation to himself and then jabbed his right fist into his left palm. And to Procopio he turned and asked, "Just where is this apparition?"

"At the wall, Your Excellency," Father Procopio said, "right by where the ugly dog is sitting."

The Bishop tried to shoo Amandito's dog away from the

wall by stomping his feet but the dog recognized the Bishop and growled and refused to move. The Bishop picked up a rock and threw it at the dog as La Poochie barked from behind the Bishop's legs. "That's right, Poochie," the Bishop praised her. "Get that ugly mean dog. Let me throw another rock at him and see if he doesn't move."

La Poochie stayed behind the Bishop, clawing at the dirt to show everyone that she had finished her business and was now in the process of running off Amandito's dog. The experienced dog saw the odds against him and he went quietly to the back of the church.

Now that the dangerous dog was gone, La Poochie contentedly followed the Bishop's every step, proud to belong to the Bishop, disgusted that she had to come to such an insignificant town and have to put up not only with the cats and the fleas, but now with a mongrel dog in her own yard. It was at moments like this that she wished she could talk to her master.

Amandito's dog had not left entirely. Instead he had gone to hide under the pomegranates to observe this strange little creature with the bashed-in face and bulging eyes that always came with the Bishop. He looked at the Bishop and then at La Poochie and wondered how they ever became related.

"And this is where the apparition appears?" the Bishop asked as he ran his hand on the wall.

"Yes, Your Excellency," Father Procopio informed him.

"And where is it now? Where is the apparition?"

"I've made it disappear," Father Procopio admitted.

The Bishop touched the wall and shook his head in disgust. "This, good Father Procopio, could mean a fortune for the church . . . for the railroad . . . for the town. Just think of it."

Father Procopio had remained by the shade of the rectory and from there he said, "It would be a lie, Your Excellency."

The Bishop felt of the wall and then checked the palm of his hand. "So?" he murmured, dusting one hand with the other.

"I couldn't put up with that," Father Procopio said.

"It's God-sent," the Bishop replied as he thought and walked over to where Father Procopio stood.

"I don't believe that," Father Procopio replied. "I must insist on showing you what the problem has been."

"What if I refuse to go with you?" the Bishop asked him as he picked up his dog.

"You'll go," Father Procopio told him. "You know that you can't live in a lie."

The Bishop looked at the good Father and raising one of his large thick eye-brows corrected him. He said, "It's been done before, Procopio. It's been done before."

Procopio, jiggling his eyebrows, braced himself as he saw Amandito's dog stand up from under the pomegranates and begin to walk away, growling. "I won't allow the apparition anymore," he informed the Bishop.

"In that case," the Bishop said, "I may have some bad news for you. . . . But let me see what you've discovered. It's the least I can do, Procopio . . . the least I can do before I relieve you of this church."

Father Procopio swallowed the thick spittle that had accumulated at the back of his throat. He had not anticipated that the Bishop would be so quick to condemn him. He said, "I didn't know that the apparition meant this much to you, Your Excellency."

"That's your trouble, good Father," the Bishop smiled, stroking his beloved Pug. "You don't know where to make your stand. Now let's see the strength of your convictions. Do we go along with the lie or do we tell the truth?"

In the attic Father Procopio showed the Bishop his dog's bed. The Bishop placed his dog on the floor and asked her to go smell the bed, and La Poochie, knowing more than the Bishop, refused to go near the pillow. "It's all right, Poochie," the Bishop said to her, "it's a feather pillow like the one you use in Corpus. Don't be afraid." But La Poochie knew what was in store for her. She could see the fleas that the Bishop didn't. The Bishop, trying to help ease her fears shoved the little dog's face into the pillow and she felt the barrage of starving fleas attack her pugged nose.

Father Procopio was nervously moving more boxes out of the way to allow the Bishop, in his white frock, to get into the back of the attic without dirtying his habit. The Bishop had let go of his dog and was waiting for Father Procopio to clear the way.

"This is where the mystery is," Father Procopio said as he cleared the last box and invited the Bishop to come in. "Right here," he said as he walked and stood between the two windows.

The Bishop looked at the good Father and said, "What are you talking about?"

Father Procopio, heavily worried about losing his church, looked around and said, "Well, Your Excellency, you can't see it now. The sun is overhead. But in the mornings, when the sun clears the salt cedars, sunlight strikes this window and the bottles on the ledge. Somehow the light is filtered and condensed and a very intense beam is created. This thin beam goes across the room here and goes to the opposite window and goes through this old bottle of hair-oil. From here the image is projected, just like a projector at the movies, down to the wall below. Naturally, as the sun travels overhead the image moves farther and farther down on the wall. By eleven in the morning the image disappears."

The Bishop stood silently for a while and looked back to find his dog. He picked up La Poochie and stroked the top of her head. "And . . . and how did this all come about, good Father?" he asked.

"Pimena," Father Procopio shrugged. "She cleaned the bottles and set them up just as you see them."

"Divine Providence," the Bishop said, smiling.

Father Procopio jiggled his eyebrows three times and the thought of losing his church became secondary to his principles. "If this is Divine Providence then it's not worth it for me to stay in this parish anymore," he said.

"As you wish," the Bishop said, shaking his head at the disloyal Priest. "And by the way, good Father," he continued, "now that the rectory is mine once more, I will sleep in your room. It's much more comfortable than the one you always give me. I just hope that your room is not as heavily infested with bedbugs as the bed you always give me."

Father Procopio swallowed the new white froth that had formed in back of his throat during his ordeal and replied, "Whatever you say, Your Excellency."

"And," the Bishop added, "I'll just have Poochie sleep with me instead of having the poor dog sleep with all of your cats."

"I'll be sure and tell Pimena about the arrangements when she returns," Father Procopio replied.

"I was just thinking," the Bishop said as he stroked his chin, "that as adamant as you are about destroying the apparition, I am going to forbid you to come into this attic anymore."

Father Procopio sighed and asked in desperation, "And my cats?"

The Bishop checked La Poochie's eyes and wiped the mucus from them and rubbed it off against one of the boxes. "They," he said, "can sleep wherever they please."

"They love to sleep in the attic, Your Excellency," Father Procopio replied.

"Very well," the Bishop concluded, "they can sleep here. But I forbid you from coming into this attic. I don't want you forcing your idealistic, your iconoclastic ways by destroying the apparition. Early in the morning I will come in this place and I will be sure that the apparition appears on the wall. Do you understand, Father Procopio?"

"Yes, Your Excellency. Whatever you say," Father Procopio answered.

"Where's your fight now, Procopio?" the Bishop sneered. "Where is your strength?"

"My strength is within me, with my Savior," the good Father responded. "I don't need to show it off."

"What will you do without a church? Where will you go?" the Bishop whispered as he stroked his beloved dog.

Father Procopio jiggled his eyebrows and said, "I'll go wherever I'm sent."

"I'm going to send you," the Bishop said with a hatred born of the glee of seeing Father Procopio defeated, "where I've never sent anyone before. It'll take me a while to figure out where but I'll figure it out. You'll see, Procopio."

Pimena returned exhausted as the Bishop and Father Procopio were sitting in the darkened kitchen without saying a word. She greeted the Bishop with much fanfare, kneeling and kissing his ring.

"Oh, Your Excellency, I'm sorry that I was not here to greet you when you arrived. But we had such a scare."

The Bishop smiled and said, lying, "I saw you, Pimena. I saw you running at the head of the pack."

"You did?" Pimena wondered. "Where were you, Your Excellency?"

"Why on my way to the rectory, Pimena," the Bishop laughed.

"Heaven and earth," she said. "I never saw you. Here, let me make you some coffee.

"I would love that," the Bishop replied, "since Father Procopio has not even offered me a glass of water."

"Shame on you, Father Procopio," Pimena scolded him as she began to take out the parts of the old coffee pot. "The least we can do is make the Bishop comfortable. . . . How long are you staying, Your Excellency?" she asked.

"It depends," the Bishop said, eyeing Father Procopio.

Pimena rinsed the coffee pot and removed the cat hairs that were stuck to the inside. "You must tell our good Father here about keeping so many cats, Your Excellency," she complained. "Look at all the cat hairs everywhere. The cats will be the ruination of all of us. Mark my words, Your Excellency."

The Bishop laughed as he put his dog down on the floor. La Poochie went over to the back door and through the screen smelled the foul odor of stale urine on Amandito's dog as he rested contentedly against the door. "I'm afraid that Father Procopio is as concerned with his twenty cats as I am with my Poochie," the Bishop said, watching proudly as La Poochie continued to smell and growl across the screen at Amandito's dog. Then to Father Procopio he asked in a whisper so that Pimena could not hear, "What are you going to do with your cats? Wherever I'm sending you, you won't be able to take them with you."

Father Procopio cupped his nervous hand over his mouth and whispered to the Bishop so that Pimena could not hear: "As long as I have my Princess, I'll be all right wherever I go."

"You must confess me, Your Excellency," Pimena told the Bishop as she faced toward the sink and filled the coffee pot with water. "You know, Your Excellency, that you are the only one that can hear my confession. As much as I love Father Procopio, I would never allow him to know my most intimate of thoughts."

The Bishop threw his large head backwards and laughed. He said, "My dear Pimena, I'm sure that Procopio has heard it all by now."

Pimena nervously put the coffee pot on the fire and finally turned on the lights. "Not from me he hasn't," she said.

The Bishop leaned toward Procopio and whispered, "I think I will send you to the farthest ranch in the deepest brush in all of south Texas."

Father Procopio jiggled his eyebrows and swallowed the spittle that had once again gathered in the back of his throat. "Whatever you say, Your Excellency," he replied, wondering what it would take to become a Protestant in order to keep his Princess and his nineteen other cats.

Over coffee the Bishop said, "Pimena, I think I will turn in early. Would you please make my bed ready?"

"We're not going to eat, Father Procopio? Surely you want me to fix supper?" Pimena asked.

"Whatever the Bishop wants, Pimena," Father Procopio said. "For my part, I'm not the least hungry."

"I'm not hungry either, Pimena," the Bishop informed her.

"Poochie's not hungry either. If she gets hungry during the night I'll get up and get her a bowl of milk."

"The bed is ready, Your Excellency," Pimena said. "I made up your bed in the small bedroom since yesterday. "

The Bishop cleared his throat and looking at Father Procopio said, "Father Procopio has been nice enough to offer me his room for my stay."

"Heaven and earth be elevated," she prayed. "It makes my heart sing to hear that both of you are on such good terms."

"Don't jump to any conclusions, Pimena," the Bishop warned her before she could further express her joy. "Right, Father Procopio?"

Father Procopio took some coffee and thought of his mother and her eternal belt. He felt his beloved Princess rub against his leg and he picked her up and began to stroke her. Amandito's dog, peering inside through the screen door, saw Princess being picked up; he barked twice and let out a sorrowful moan that scared La Poochie back into the Bishop's lap.

"You make a sight," Pimena said, surveying the two men at the table. "Such important men with a dog and cat on their laps."

"We're putty in the hands of these wonderful little animals," the Bishop said as he kissed La Poochie on the top of her large head.

"Pimena," Father Procopio said, admiring how much the Bishop loved his little ugly dog, "you'd better make up the bed in the small bedroom for me."

"But I already did, good Father," Pimena replied. "I made it up for His Excellency."

"No you haven't," Father Procopio said. "Go look for yourself."

"Good Father," Pimena said mildly, "if you are right then I'm ready for the house for the insane. This apparition is getting the best of me."

"Get ready to pack then," Father Procopio advised her,

secure in the knowledge that it had been he that had undone the bed to spread the bedbugs on the mattress.

At night the Bishop tossed in his bed, trying to extract the hair from twenty cats from all the areas of his body, cat hair that to Father Procopio had become an essential part of his sleep. The Bishop tried combing the cat hair from his own hair, tried to scrape cat hair from his own tongue, tried to rub it off his torso, his legs, his feet, his arms, from around his neck, from his back. Sleep was impossible. He was wishing now that he had taken the small bedroom along with the starving bedbugs that Father Procopio saved for him. He looked across the bed and could see that La Poochie was not asleep. She was having difficulty breathing with all the cat hair around her.

In the small bedroom Father Procopio said his rosary as the bedbugs feasted on his body. He could hear the Bishop across the hall cursing him and he smiled as another bedbug got him between the toes.

At precisely three in the morning, when the rectory clock struck the hour, Father Procopio, still awake and slapping at the infinitely small bedbugs, saw the Bishop through the wooden door, as he saw Pimena every morning, as the Bishop walked into the hallway, dressed in a white gown and carrying La Poochie. He heard the Bishop knock very gently. "Procopio," the Bishop whispered through the door. "Procopio . . . are you awake? I can't sleep with the infernal cat hair. You should have warned me. That was the least you could have done . . . are you awake? Procopio?"

"Yes, Your Excellency," Procopio replied, as he sat up and moved to the edge of his small bed.

"Procopio . . . We can still be friends. Be reasonable. Think of the people."

"I'm going to try to go to sleep," Father Procopio answered.

"Very well," the Bishop said. There was a long pause as the Bishop waited in vain for Father Procopio to give in. Then the Bishop sighed through the door at the good Father and walked away disappointed.

At four in the morning Father Procopio was awakened by the Bishop's noise in the hallway. He heard the mild footsteps as he saw through the wall as the Bishop walked downstairs carrying the hungry Poochie. Father Procopio lay silent, a bedbug in his ear. He cursed himself for having put all these little creatures in the Bishop's bed. God had punished him. He could hear the Bishop tripping around downstairs and the Bishop cursing the darkness. He lay very still, ignoring the bedbugs that were happily chewing at his body, trying to understand what the Bishop was doing at this hour. He could hear Poochie barking. He heard a loud noise, like a scream, but then his mind told him that it could not be a scream, that it was a cough, the Bishop clearing his throat of all the cat hair that he had swallowed during the night. He heard the noise again. And then again. And again. It was more than a cough. He distinctly heard the deep shouting voice of a man, the Bishop, as if he were talking very loudly to someone. He heard the noise made from frantic footsteps running on hard floors. He heard the running footsteps under his room, then toward his office, then back on the downstairs hallway. He heard the Bishop screaming at the top of his voice for someone to stop. He heard the panting as someone ran up the stairs. The Bishop was right behind whoever it was. At the top of the stairs he heard the Bishop scream for Father Procopio's help. Father Procopio jumped from the bed and ran to the door. He threw the door open just in time to see Amandito's dog running by the door heading for the attic. He had La Poochie clamped between his jaws. The dog hit the door with such an impact that it flew open. The Bishop, running after Amandito's dog, trying to save La Poochie's life, was so winded that he was clutching his heart and could not speak. The Bishop raised his right hand and Father Procopio saw the blood where the dog had bitten the Bishop. Father Procopio was frozen momentarily at seeing the attack on La Poochie and at seeing the blood on the Bishop's hand.

At first the good Father heard La Poochie's weak cries coming from the attic, fearful little whimpers, no longer the fierce barks that she had shown the whole town earlier in the day. She sounded near death inside the mouth of the much larger dog. Then he heard the commotion as twenty cats ran wildly around the crowded room. Father Procopio heard boxes fall, cats scream, Amandito's dog growling ferociously. The Bishop and Father Procopio ran into the attic and began chasing Amandito's dog while La Poochie screamed in pain. Amandito's dog escaped through the alley that Father Procopio had made of the boxes in order to get to the bottles. The Bishop dove at the dog as La Poochie screamed for him to save her. Father Procopio was able to grab the dog by one of the hind legs and all of them—the Bishop, Father Procopio, Amandito's dog, La Poochie,—crashed against the left window knocking down all the bottles off the ledge. Then to the right they went, the dog dragging both Father Procopio and the Bishop with an unnatural power. The snarling, howling group crashed against the right window this time and knocked the bottles off the ledge. Father Procopio, as if by Divine Intervention, finally remembered the dog's weak point. He grabbed Amandito's dog by the testicles and twisted them around and around and then yanked them up toward the tail. The dog let go of La Poochie immediately and started on Father Procopio. Father Procopio ran out, the dog in pursuit, and he flew down the stairs without touching them and ran down the hallway to the back door. He opened the door and took one step to the outside. As the dog followed right behind him, Father Procopio stopped, stepped to one side and the dog ran out past him and tumbled over the back-door steps. He yelped in pain as he rolled for several yards on the hard ground. Father Procopio jumped back inside and closed the door.

"Damn dog," he said. "Wait until I tell Amandito about you. He's going to take you and see that your testicles are removed."

He made sure that both the screen door and the wooden door were locked. At that moment, as he made sure Amandito's dog had run away, he heard the Bishop scream in agony and he ran upstairs to see what had happened. As he ran he prayed for

La Poochie's life. What would the Bishop do without her?

In the middle of the attic the Bishop, his own hand bleeding, held the bleeding Poochie to his chest and cried. Father Procopio walked slowly toward the Bishop and could see that La Poochie's whole limp body was covered with blood and saliva. As Father Procopio tried to take the dog away, the Bishop objected. He would not let the dog go. Father Procopio took the stunned Bishop by the arms and led him into the bathroom. There the two of them cleaned La Poochie under the warm stream of the sink. Her right front leg was broken. She had been bitten mostly on her head. The whites of both her little eyes were bleeding from the trauma. The Bishop collapsed by the sink, fell to his knees and began to pray as he cried. His hand had been washed when they had cleaned La Poochie and Father Procopio could see the teeth marks on the Bishop's palm.

Father Procopio worked on La Poochie all the rest of the night, stroking her, keeping her warm, exhorting her not to die, and by daybreak, when Pimena came to work, the little dog was resting comfortably under the covers made from the Bishop's nightgown. The Bishop sat on the floor by her and stroked her little head.

"What in heaven's name happened here last night?" they could hear Pimena ask. "It looks as if a hurricane slept in here. What could have happened?"

"Your Excellency," Father Procopio said to the Bishop, "we must take Poochie to the veterinarian in Alice."

"No," he said, tired and forlorn, "I need to take her as soon as possible to Corpus. To her own veterinarian where she belongs. Do you think she can travel?"

"I'm sure of it," Father Procopio replied, looking at La Poochie as she licked her wounds, as she shuddered at how close to death she had come.

"Heaven and earth," Pimena said as she walked upstairs, "look at all this mess and blood. Something sure stirred up the cat hair last night."

In one hour the Bishop had packed and was ready to leave for Corpus Christi. He and Father Procopio had made a crude splint and had wrapped La Poochie's leg.

"Pimena," the Bishop cried as he looked for the housekeeper. "Pimena, I'm leaving. Father Procopio is walking with me to the depot."

Pimena walked slowly from upstairs, crying.

"What is it, Pimena?" Father Procopio asked her. "What has happened? Why are you crying?"

Pimena wiped the tears with her apron as she walked. "Oh, good Father," she cried. "If you only knew."

"What happened, Pimena? In God's name," the Bishop demanded.

"Father Procopio," Pimena cried, "it's Princess." She began to gag but managed to get the words out. "I found her dead. A box fell on her and crushed her."

Father Procopio ran upstairs to the attic as the Bishop began to nervously run around the room. "Oh my God!" he cried. "Poor man. And it's all my fault. How he must feel!" he said as he stopped and thought about Father Procopio. He ran around the room some more as Pimena tried to quiet him down.

Upstairs, they heard the cries of Father Procopio as he gazed at the crushed Princess for the first time. "She's dead!" they could hear him cry. "She's dead . . . all that I had is dead. Why is God so cruel?"

The Bishop, on hearing the screams of the Priest upstairs, ran for his dog and cradled it in his arm. With the other hand he picked up his luggage and hurriedly ran for the door. There was no use staying there for the aftermath.

As he held the door open with his foot he said: "Pimena, tell the good Father that I couldn't wait. Tell him how I feel for him. Offer condolences . . . anything. How the poor man must feel . . . Tell him to forget about the apparition. Tell him that whatever he wants to do is fine with me. Tell him he's right . . . as always."

Pimena had never seen the old Bishop move as fast as he did that morning. Both fascinated and repulsed by his speed, she had not had time to reply. By the time she had collected her thoughts the Bishop was a black blur running up the street toward town and the train depot. In his right arm he carried the injured dog and dangling from his left hand, like a tow sack, was his patent leather bag.

Two weeks later Father Procopio received the letter from the Bishop. La Poochie's bite wounds had healed. Her little crooked leg had been set and placed in a cast. She was able to take short walks. He could tell that she hurt because she would bark at him after a few blocks and he would have to pick her up and carry her the rest of the way. His hand was healing nicely but he had had to be vaccinated against tetanus just as La Poochie had. He had just one complaint about San Diego: Father Procopio should not allow the old man, the one known as Don Tomas, to loiter at the depot. It was bad enough that Don Tomas had bothered him when he first arrived from Corpus Christi but waiting for the train as he had had to do was too much. The old man had pestered the Bishop unmercifully. The Bishop wrote: "In the condition that La Poochie and I were in, I did not appreciate anyone asking me if I knew that snakes have sexual intercourse like dogs and whether I knew that the possum breeds through the nose, that coyotes defecate on their young and in particular I don't care, nor does the Almighty God care, whether the spider pees or not. But nothing I could say or do could convince the man to leave me alone. P.S.: How is the congregation taking to the loss of the apparition?"

Father Procopio jiggled his eyebrows for the hundredth time since he had found Princess's crushed body in the attic. He took a pen and paper and wrote: "Your Excellency: I am happy for you and La Poochie and expect that she will be back to normal in a short time. Take care of your hand. You know what happened to Father Diaz at Alton when he did not take care of his bite wound and he had to be hospitalized and almost lost his arm. For Your Excellency's information, I had Bernabe, the crazy one, bury Princess by the side of the church where I used to see her sleeping during the day. You will be happy to know that Amandito and I took the dog to Alice and had him castrated as per Don Andres Garcia's death-bed instructions. I have not seen him around the rectory since. P.S.: The loss of the apparition has not deterred the ladies of the congregation. They are even more devout now than before, coming to pray at the wall instead of inside the church. You can imagine what that does to the collection plate! What's more, they are eagerly expecting another apparition very soon. You can tell, Your Excellency, that I did not have the heart to tell them the truth."

Judith Ortiz Cofer

Judith Ortiz Cofer is the author of numerous award-winning books, including children's books and poetry. Her titles include *An Island Like You: Stories of the Barrio*, *Terms of Survival*, and *Reaching for the Mainland*. Her memoir *Silent Dancing* received a PEN Special Citation and was named a Best Book for the Teen Age by the New York Public Library.

Gravity

My bedroom was my inner sanctum where I kept my books, my radio—which was always on when I was there—and the other symbols of my rebellion: tie-dye T-shirts, Indian headbands and jewelry that made music when I moved; a stick of patchouli incense burning on its wooden stand. My mother decorated the rest of the place in what I referred to as Early Puerto Rican: a religious print in every room. I had removed my Guardian Angel from my wall, the one depicting a winged creature in flowing robes leading a little girl and boy over the rickety bridge. (The children appeared to be as oblivious to their guardian as to the dark abyss opening up beneath them.) I was taking a stand by refusing to decorate with angels and saints, and by disdaining everything my parents loved. My mother put the picture up in the hallway, right in front of my bedroom door so that I'd have to see it coming in and out. It came to be a symbol for me of our relationship in those days.

Evenings she'd sit in her rocking chair in the living room and listen to record albums she bought on the Island during our yearly visits to her mother's home: Celia Cruz, Felipe Rodriguez, and the big band music of Tito Puente, which she played loud to compete with my Little Richard, the Supremes, Dylan and, later, the Beatles, the Beatles, the Beatles. When my father came home we both turned down the volume. He had to listen to the *vellonera,* a monstrous juke-box going all day long at the restaurant where he worked for the "magnanimous" Mr. Larry Reyes. My mother and father thought everything he did was inspired, including naming the place Puerto Habana to please both his Puerto Rican and Cuban clientele. Papi had to endure listening to the same popular records played over and over by the regulars. When he came home he expected two things: that the music be kept down and that we all sit down to dinner together.

167

It was my clothes that visibly upset him. He could not keep himself from staring at my waist-long hair worn loose and wild but encircled, for decoration, by a headband embroidered in Navajo designs. I also wore bell-bottom blue jeans torn and faded just right, and the orange sunburst tie-dye T-shirts, once his undershirts, in fact, which I had borrowed from the clothesline to experiment with. This is how I was dressed on New Year's Eve, 1965. In my room, Dylan's "The Times They Are A-Changin'" ' was playing softly on the radio.

I knew that my rebel disguise worried my parents, but we had an unspoken agreement we all understood would be revoked if they objected too much to my hippie clothes and loud music. By day I looked and acted like a good Catholic girl, wearing my Queen of Heaven High School uniform of gray plaid wool, penny-loafers with socks, hair in a braid, the whole bit. After school I became whoever and whatever I wanted.

I felt that the sacrifice of my ideals for eight hours was worth it to be around Sister Mary Joseph, the counter-culture nun who fed us revolutionary literature and Eastern philosophy under the guise of teaching English literature. I was getting an excellent education at the Catholic school although I felt no more a part of the mostly Irish student body than I had at Public School Number 16 in my barrio, among "my own kind." But at Queen of Heaven I was at least free from barrio pressures, even if never asked to join the sororities or invited to parties. And even this was changing as the Movement infected the clean-cut crowds. Sister Mary Joseph had started a café in an unused basement room where on Fridays, four or five of us hairier students met with her to listen to the exotic records she brought—music to feed our souls: Gregorian chants, Tibetan drums and bells, poets reading their doomsday verses in funereal tones to the rhythms of lyres. We sat in the lotus position and meditated or talked excitedly about "the Revolution."

I had fallen for one of the boys, a tall, thin, black-haired nascent poet named Gerald who wore a purple beret that matched the dark circles under his eyes. He looked like my idea of a poet. He would later become known in our crowd for being the only one among us to go to Woodstock. The trip would cost him: LSD would leave him so disconnected that he would have to spend six months in a "home." But the aura of the "event" he would bring back was perhaps worth the high price to Gerald—we'd remember him as the only one among us who witnessed the phenomenon of Woodstock firsthand. But that was still years away. When I had my crush on him, Gerald's rebellion was still in its pupal stage. At school we shared our poems and fueled each other's intensity.

Our cafe was at first scorned by the other kids. Then, perhaps because our little group was self-sufficient, even the popular kids asked about what we did in the basement and wanted to be taken there. Once we opened it up to the "others," the club lost some of its intimacy and mystery, but it widened the circle of my social life too.

I could never ask any of my friends over to our apartment. They would have suffered culture shock. So I divided myself into two people—actually three, if you counted the after-school hippie version as a separate identity. It was not always easy to shuffle out of my visionary self and into the binding coat of propriety the Puerto Rican girl was supposed to wear, although my parents were more understanding than others in our barrio.

That New Year's Eve, we were supposed to attend the annual party at the restaurant, Puerto Habana. That meant my father would be stuck behind the bar serving Budweisers and rum-and-cokes all night. My mother would play hostess for the owner, Mr. Reyes, who would be busy accepting everyone's gratitude and good wishes. I knew I was not dressed appropriately for the occasion, but I was looking to expand my horizons in the new year with a few new brazen acts of rebellion.

"Elenita," my mother began as she cleared the table, "did you forget about the fiesta tonight?"

"No, Maria Elena, I did not forget about the fiesta to-night." (I had also decided to call my mother by her first name as an experiment in "evolving" our roles.)

She frowned at me, but said nothing about it. I suspected that she and my father had "strategized" about how best to handle me. "Just ignore her. It's a stage. It will pass, you'll see," I could just hear them saying to each other.

"Then why are you not dressed?"

"I am dressed, Maria Elena. I'm not naked, am I?"

"How about that pretty green taffeta dress we bought you for Honors Day?"

That horrible mistake of a dress was in the back of my closet. My mother had insisted we buy it when I had won a cer-tificate for an essay I had written in English class: "Brave New World For Women." Sister Mary Joseph had been one of the judges. My mother had, bought me a party dress to wear to school that day. I had worn it into the girls' lavatory, where I had promptly changed to a plain black skirt and white blouse.

"It's too small for me now. Maybe you haven't noticed but I have breasts now."

She dropped a tin pot noisily into the sink and faced me. I had said *breasts* in front of my father. She knew I was deliber-ately provoking her.

He, in the meantime, had gulped down the last of his cof-fee and hurriedly kissed her cheek, exiting. "I'll be waiting for you at Puerto, *querida*. I promised *el Señor* Reyes I would open early. Please be careful walking there. The sidewalks are icy," he said, without looking at me. He knew how I felt about his boss, the imperialist Lorenzo, *alias* Larry Reyes.

For the greater part of my childhood I had practically lived with my parents at Puerto Habana. My father opened and dosed the restaurant: twelve-hour days. And my mother was always on stand-by, as cook, waitress, hostess, whatever Reyes needed; al-most every day, she was needed. My father thought of the restau-rant as the heart of his barrio life. On the other hand, Mami talked constantly about the family on the Island. It was point-counterpoint every day, not quite an argument, just an ongoing discussion about where "home" was for each of them.

Papi's reasons for not going back to Puerto Rico with us varied from year to year: Not the right time, not enough money, he was needed here by Mr. Reyes. It was only years later that I learned through my mother's stories that Jorge was ashamed of the fact that he could not provide for us the kinds of luxuries my mother had had growing up in a middle-class family in Puerto Rico. He felt rejected by her mother and scorned by his successful brother-in-law. His—our—lower middle-class status, actually more like middle working-class level, did not bother him any other time, however. When he talked about Puerto Habana, his job there which allowed him contact with just about everyone in our barrio, he sounded proud. Every other sentence began with his benefactor's name, Larry Reyes. Larry Reyes plans to open the restaurant after regular hours to serve a special free meal *para los mayores*, for the old people. Larry Reyes is sending baskets to the sick ones who cannot come to Puerto Habana. Every week Larry Reyes had a new scheme which my father committed himself to, heart and soul, and free time. He would be there to serve the old people after regular hours. And he and Mother would get his old black Buick out of its parking spot in the back of the restaurant and ride to decrepit places all over town delivering sandwiches and hot *asopao*, chicken soup Puerto Rican style, in thermos jugs to everyone on Reyes's list.

Sometimes I would go with them and sit in the cold car rather than go into dark hallways that smelled of urine and other unimaginable human waste and decay. My mother often came out with tears in her eyes. On the way home she would tell us stories of how she and her mother had also delivered food and medicines in Puerto Rico during the war: "But it was never like this, Jorge. The poor on the island did not live in this kind of filth. There was the river to bathe in, if there was no plumbing. There was a garden to grow a few things. They would not starve

171

as long as they had a little plot of earth. Jorge, this is not living!"
And she would sob a little. His arm would be around her shoulders. He would kiss her on the forehead and talk about how good
it was to be able to help people, even in a small way.

Yeah, right, I'd be thinking, huddled in the back seat, the
poor people of her dream island didn't have the swollen bellies
of malnutrition I had read about in books, nor did they have to
drink the putrid waters of rivers now polluted with human and
industrial waste in the famous slums of her island paradise. My
irritation at my parents' naiveté grew along with my suspicion of
Reyes's acts of charity.

Reyes was an easier target for my self-righteous anger
than my parents, whom I saw as victims of his schemes. I be-
lieved that he was doing these things for himself. He saw himself
as the Don in our barrio, the businessman-philanthropist. Yet he
never got his hands dirty dealing with the poor. It was always my
mother's heart that broke, and my father's back. And our family
time that was usurped. I resolved to get out of this system of
haves, have-nots and in-betweens that dominated our lives in the
barrio. I learned about the feudal system of king, lords and peas-
ants in my history class, and I thought I saw a clear analogy between the barrio structure and the Middle Ages. I would not be
trapped in this web of deceit with the capitalist Reyes as the fat
spider in the middle.

Since I didn't even have a driver's license yet, my revolt
was at that time limited to small acts of defiance, like the one I
had planned to execute that New Year's Eve, to let at least my
mother know where I stood.

"Elena. Why are you so fresh? If you are a *señorita* as
you are always telling me, why don't you act like one?"

But it was she who was always reminding me to act like a
señorita, which meant the opposite to her of what I thought. I felt
I was an adult, or at least on the verge. To her it meant that I was
to act more *decente.* Sit right so that your underwear doesn't show
under your miniskirt, do not mention sex or body parts in front of

men—not even your own father—don't do this, don't do that. To me being fifteen meant that I should be allowed at least to choose my own clothes, my own friends, and to say whatever I wanted to say when I wanted to say it—free country, right?

"Maybe I won't go to this party." I had no wish to socialize with the barrio's matrons and their over-dressed daughters, nor to dance with older men, including Reyes, whose breath stank of rum and cigarettes and who would be crying like babies at the stroke of midnight, "¡Ay mi Cuba! ¡Ay mi Borinquén!" All calling out for their islands, and shedding tears for their old mamás who waited in their casas for their hijos to come home. Actually, though I would never have admitted it then, I loved the dancing and the food, and especially listening to the women tell dirty jokes at their tables while the men played dominoes and got drunk at theirs. But I had taken my battle position.

"Está bien, hija."

She caught me totally by surprise when she said in a sad, resigned voice that I could do as I wished.

"You are old enough to stay here alone. I have to help Jorge." She left me at the kitchen table, defeated by her humble acceptance of my decision when I had hoped for a little fight— one that I could have graciously finally lost—though I was firm on the matter of the puke-green taffeta dress.

Minutes later she emerged from her room looking like a Mexican movie star. She wore a tight-fitting black satin dress with a low neck, showing off her impressive bosom—which made me ashamed to have brought up the subject of my negligible little buds. She had her hair up in a French twist to show off the cameo earrings her Jorge had given her for Christmas. Maria Elena was still a beautiful woman—though hopelessly behind the times.

"Lock the door behind me, will you, Elenita," she said, her voice soft and sad. I nodded as she walked away without a glance back at me.

An hour or so later I found myself looking through my closet for a reasonable compromise between taffeta and denim.

As always on New Year's Eve, my father asked me to dance the last dance of the year with him, and at midnight he held my mother as she wept in his arms for her *isla* and her *familia* so far away. This time I did not just feel my usual little pang of jealousy for being left out of their perceptions. Seeing the way she held on to him, and how he placed his lips on her tear-streaked face as if to absorb her grief, I felt a need awakening in me, a sort of hunger to connect with someone of my own. One minute into the new year—the beginning of the year of my revolution—and it had nothing to do with the times, but with time's only gift to us: the love that binds us: its gravitational pull.

Stephen D. Gutierrez

The Happening: A Storytelling Event

[So he sits on a stool strumming a few licks, composing a few lyrics to himself as the band scurries around him. The band is made up of a few vagrants he's thrust instruments upon and told to play, man, play.

And then he warms up on this fine sunny day in Northern Califas, a day when the sun has peeked out and fooled El Niño of the torrential rains with a dew-bedecked smile. Everything's wet.

His foot is wet, bouncing to the beat of his song.

The trousers of the players are wet.

The equipment is wet.

And if you look up high enough up to the warehouse ceiling of studio number 9 (a safely discreet tucked away in the cavernous hills of Northern California retreat some shitheads claim is a garage), you see the wet spots on the interior roof soaking through.

Big, fat drops of rain fall down between riffs, and thus they call us (I'm just the manager), The Wetbacks Extempore, this day of jamming and improvising in my recently decked-out and retrofitted place of sound and management, man.]

"Helen's Song, man," singing, singing, "Helen's Song."

He starts out with that tune he's been playing all morning, launching into the guitar and face-forwarding the microphone in a bold move of cara larga, tragic and doleful.

"This is about a little girl named Helen, man."

And then he goes on with a soft refrain:

"Helen's Song, man, I'm singing 'bout Helen's Song, man."

And from the side I shout encouragement, "Pick it up, man," because I don't want any long drawn-out José Feliciano on reds thing doing a cover of The Doors or something when we would have a voz of the people here, now, in the studio talking to

177

the masses about something important, La Raza and where we all be at now.

I'm down.

And actually José (my friend and business associate from way back) was down on that one.

Might even have out Jimmed Jim if it wasn't for the slight excessive rendering of the final lyrics that brought up short in my estimation.

"Pick it up, man, slow and easy, hard and driving." I give him a consonance of variables to work with within my ultimate parameters of range.

I sweep the floor with a mike picking up dissonance.

"Okay, Gutiérrez, el Jefe," he shouts back from the stage giving me a wayward nod.

"¿Qúe onda?" the vato says, right in the middle of his song.

And then the Wetbacks go into action.

They step forward.

Wetback Number One (Uno) aggravates the playing space in the middle of the stage with his homemade guitarra of ultra guitarrón parts and shiny Schwinn sprockets putting together a mighty fine sound, Chicano and down.

He's down to the bone.

He's bad.

"Es la Helen, man, era la Helen," he admits to the mike.

So we picked the vato up off the streets and he doesn't really know Spanish but that's all right too, eh?

He goes on: "Es la Helen, man, era la Helen back in the old days."

"Back in the old days, see," Number Two, El Dos, comes on top of him and sings into the mike with might.

"Helen's Song, man," singing, singing, "Helen's Song," they go down together before breaking up.

They go down to the waters, man, the waters.

"Helen's Song, man," singing, singing, "Helen's Song."

"And we go way back, we went way back," Dos picks up

the story where it counts, holding a brass trumpet at his side.

He thumps his thigh with the mouth of the brass trumpet.

And up above the flanged lips of the brass trumpet a brass belt buckle big and round proclaims Michoacan, Mexico, but when he turns around, on his back is proclaimed Pico Rivera, California (Ellay), and when he spins around you can't tell which one is which where.

He's just a spinning, whirling dervish of carnalismo and Sam Peckinpah revenge.

He shoots up the studio with a spitting trumpet, mariachi-style.

Pa pa pa.

And then he's back at the mike with his song: "Era la Helen, man, from way back."

"Sí, era la Helen." Number One can't help but play some guitarra now.

The Schwinn sprockets help.

"Helen's Song, man," singing, singing, "Helen's Song."

Walter Ramirez, lead man for The Wetbacks Extempore, leads.

He bursts forth with the following refrain joyfully leading the crowd: "Helen's Song, man," singing, singing, "Helen's Song."

And then he goes on into his song: "It was back in the old days at Bell Gardens Junior High School in the good old town of Bell Gardens down South way that I met a girl named Helen Boas, man, and fell in love." He turns around for effect.

He wants to know if the two Wetbacks behind him have heard him.

He wants call and response.

"Sí, como qúe no, go on."

And the beat goes on, a combination of early Santana enclosed by a new Chicano sound alternately dystopic and yearning, heartfelt and vengeful but opening up into new spaces of sorrow and hunger.

A barely contained discordancy threatens collapse.

But the hopelessness of the rhythm is relieved by an ancient Mexican wisdom perpetuated through smoking drum kettles booming a magnificent sepulchral beat to the cadence of a more upbeat, slightly melancholy mariachi tune.

Old mariachis walk around and then disappear.

The best of their sound lingers, and the ancient Aztec drums boom on.

"Helen's Song, man," singing, singing, "Helen's Song."

And the song moves forward.

And Walter goes on to say, "And so I went on to fall in love with this Helen Boas," and he shakes his head negatively looking so much like a young José Feliciano that José Feliciano shows up and claps.

"And all night long we did it!"

"Man, keep it real!" The Wetbacks bump heads rushing to the mike, not putting up with any of this bullshit, the brothers.

"So okay we didn't," he admits and backs down with a José Feliciano smile on his face, the same shades two sizes too small hiked up on his nose.

He wears Converse tennis shoes out of style three years ago and Gap pants he thinks are cool.

They have buttons down the side.

But everybody's grooving and things like clothes don't count in the new world.

"Helen's Song, man," singing, singing, "Helen's Song."

The Wetbacks behind him jump in with the refrain, looking at the floor in astonishment as puddles of water rise up to their knees.

Before both Wetbacks their ancestors cross in a rushing river rising above their heads. Swallowed up, they disappear in the turbulent waters thrusting hands on.

They shout out in garbled Spanish: "Remember us! Remember us!"

And Wetback Number Two, Dos, spins around so fast you can't see him.

But when he stops his belt buckle is clear: Pico Rivera, California (Ellay) shines forth in red, white and blue overtones with only the hint of green underneath.

He screams into the mike: "I ain't no fucking wetback!"

And then both Wetbacks pause before starting again.

"My people," they read from a script handed to them by an in-rushing man.

The man bears a curious resemblance to a rival promoter trying to overthrow me and my sound.

"They came here legally in the teens," they continue with their best-intoned confident beliefs. "They walked across the fucking border sometimes!"

"Or even took the train." Wetback Number Two beseeches understanding as the tide of water washes over his heavily buck-led waist and drowns him.

And then they all go on out of nowhere.

"Helen's Song, man," singing, singing, "Helen's Song."

Walter steps forward and lays down the law.

"We're all fucking wetbacks! Always have been!"

The Wetbacks two spy each other as if they're caught.

Then they bust up laughing, and the band plays harder and better than ever.

"Helen's Song, man," singing, singing, "Helen's Song."

And they shake their heads in amazement over the fact that they are wetbacks now and forever now.

"Helen's Song, man," singing, singing, "Helen's Song," explodes forth out of them with Walter in charge.

The Wetbacks Extempore back him fully.

"So I fell in love with this little girl."

"Say it, man, say it."

"And we went skating together, man, at the Pico Rivera Rollerdrome."

"I know it, man, I know it!"

"And we held hands, man!" He throws his head back and catches the sun-torn roof of the studio mistaken for a garage by some.

"Helen's Song, man," singing, singing, "Helen's Song."
"And we made love!"

[Cut it! Cut it! Cut it!" So I have to rush in to put a check on this thing. My voice, after all, is the controlling one, and who am I to abuse my power of control and moderation in such a venture of wild, upended power and force? Some decorousness is demanded, and I demand it. What I want, I get. "Cut the fucking bullshit! Stick to the story clean and cut the fucking bullshit! Take a walk home!" I shout through a bullhorn at the Wetbacks.

Raging rivers attempt to engulf me but I wade away. "Get to it, Wetbacks!"]

"Helen's Song, man," singing, singing, "Helen's Song."
And the band plays on.

They sing together in unison.

"I was in love, and I had a crush on a seventh grader named Helen Boas, and she had a sweater, man, a black sweater, that was actually mine, that she wore all year long because I lent her that sweater, man, and even though I don't have that sweater no more," Walter the man grabs the mike from his stool.

Eyes closed, he's the picture of soul, man, soul. "No more, I say no more! Even though she don't have it no more. . . ."

"I mean I want to put it like this to you, people." He's an old time hood newly reformed and repentant. "If I did, man, if I did . . ."

And the band plays on.

"I would smell it."

"Helen's Song, man," singing, singing, "Helen's Song."
And the band plays on far into the night.

And he sings that same old song of innocent love, heart-breakingly plain, sweet and simple.

"Helen's Song, man," singing, singing, "Helen's Song."
"And then later, man, and then later. . . ."
Dark shadows cross the lawn of studio number 9.

"Helen's Song, man," singing, singing, "Helen's Song."
I prowl around outside.

The song goes on.

The Wetbacks are in full swing.

They're competently acclimated and adjusted to each other.

On their backs are Mexico-shaped maps soaked into their jackets with blazing stars in their home states.

Carlos Santana nods his head in the wings as I walk in.

He gives me a brief nod and curtails his involvement when I suggest a new contract with Esteban David Gutiérrez Productions.

Producciónes Azul de la Tierra Aztlán is what I underline my self with.

"No, man, I'm pretty wrapped up in my own thing nowadays." And then he's out the door into Santana night, and I'm remembering the excitement of his first three albums when he caught better than anybody since the sound of a Chicano soul plain and wailing, beautiful, plangent and tragic.

"Helen's Song, man," singing, singing, "Helen's Song."

And he plays on.

"'Bout a woman named Helen I heard about in El Fresno one of these days in the not so distant past."

"Helen's Song, man," singing, singing, "Helen's Song."

And The Wetbacks Extempore play on.

They play on hard and driving and musical and beautiful and brilliant.

They accompany the saddest of songs.

"About a ruca named Helen."

"Helen's Song, man," singing, singing, "Helen's Song."

"Who was so bad, so fine, so lost," the three join in.

"She was on heroin, man," Walter caps the song.

The refrain goes on: "She was on heroin, man."

The Wetbacks Extempore sing, "Heroin, heroin, heroin," to the rain-soaked roof for a minute or two, and then they get down on their knees and pray to the rhythm of the great kettle drums beating out Aztec cadences behind them, crossing themselves in traditional fashion after their grandparents who came across the river so many years ago in tow.

"My great-grandparents came, man."

"Shut up!"

And then el Walter begins again.

"Heroin, man, is destroying the people." They bow their heads down and cry.

"Great god in heaven release us from heroin!" Walter shouts to the sky.

"Drinking!"

"Don't be so severe, ay." Number Uno shoots him a fierce look, and Walter just cries breaking down on the stage right there.

"Helen's Song, man," singing, singing, "Helen's Song."

["Wrap it up, man, wrap it up, bring it to a close," I step forward out of the dark-shadowed wings, Carlos Santana hand-kerchief in my pocket, doing a little two-step baile to keep the music going while the music's going but wanting to end this thing now and drain my patio.

I must admit my studio is pushed far back from my house and things get clogged up in the rainy season. The hills are alive with music, and then I see the Von Trapps skirting down the montaña behind me and I want out.

Behind them are Nazis led by Pete Wilson in a beneficent uniform of powder blue and tassels.

"We love you!" he shouts.

And then I remember I support him in everything he does and really don't want to hang around here anymore.

I want them out, out.

"Out," I say, pointing my finger. "Out!"

I make throat-cutting gestures to indicate cut, cut, cut.

"Cut!"

But do they listen to me?

Nah. They go on playing.]

"Helen's Song, man," singing, singing, "Helen's Song."

[Because another concern of mine is that Wetbacks fans

from all over the world might show up any minute now and cross over the great divide of water logging my backyard, and find themselves in the sacrosanct space of my studio sometimes called a garage, and then what am I gonna do to feed the multitudes?]

"Who's gonna feed the people, man?"

The Wetbacks Extempore turn on me fiercely.

"Helen's Song, man," singing, singing, "Helen's Song!"

[And I disappear into the wings again waiting to get this damn thing over with. The thought of Wetbacks fans converging on my space from all over the world bothers me. What would they do with such a new song? Play with it till it ain't no more again?

I want lunch and I want a tight song, man.]

"Helen's Song, man," singing, singing, "Helen's Song."

And they all assume their respective positions on stage.

Walter is El Primer Chico, center stage, and Numero Uno and Numero Does flank him.

They stand behind him.

They beat rhythm against their knees with tambourines.

The kettle drums pound out the song.

"Helen's Song," sounds in Nahuatl.

Nobody stops to listen because everybody is just too busy grooving on Carlos Santana passing out flyers to his next concert.

Sam Peckinpah screens a new film of stupid Mexicans dying gruesomely and realistically, and all the filmmakers from the eighties jack off in a row.

Jissom coats the walls.

"Helen's Song, man," singing, singing, "Helen's Song."

[Walter mounts a buffalo on center stage and sings with a hand-held microphone to his lips. When he wants to, he gets down and sings in Tony Bennett style.

He's good, bad, stylish, polished.

His pants have become unbuttoned and show his ancient brown thigh tasty and sweat-glistening.]

"Helen's Song, man," singing singing, "Helen's song."

Walter stands forth among all the people singing.

"Say it, man, say it," the Wetbacks two encourage him.

And Walter leans down low and spits into the mike, "Was a woman named Helen, was . . ."

"Yes?"

"A heroin addict named Helen, was . . ."

"Yes!"

"A ruca de aquellas named Helen. I heard her name, oh yes." Walter reaches up real high to show the crowd he believes, waving his hand in a fluttery way that convinces some to boo, others to exit, and others to stand on their feet and applaud rapturously.

"And I saw her!"

"Yes?"

"Walking down the street in Fresno!"

"Helen's Song, man," singing, singing, "Helen's Song, man."

"And she was wearing garters."

"Yes?"

"And she stunk and smelled of sex."

"Yes?"

"And she is all of us here gathered today you me and everyone here gathered today she was and is all of us."

"Amen, brother!"

"Sing it!"

"Helen's Song, man," singing, singing, "Helen's Song."

"And before we forget that all, oh," Walter drops to one knee and extends a hand to the audience.

Millions of Wetbacks fans crowd among each other wanting to be close.

"Helen's Song, man," singing, singing, "Helen's Song."

"And then where would we be then what?" He rolls his head up in a cockeyed view of the heaven-hiding ceiling waterlogged and ready to burst, asking that simple question: "And then where would we be then, what?"

"If we forget about our little girlfriend?" The two

Wetbacks jump in conjuring up Helen Boas who walks onstage after handing Walter's sweater to him.

"Helen's Song, man," singing, singing, "Helen's Song, man."

And he takes that sweater and rolls in it on the dirt floor of my studio, crying and suffocating himself with its sweet-smelling warmth.

Carlos Santana floats in from the audience and starts playing a crazy and terrible and urgent melody never before released.

Behind him the two Wetbacks bow their heads and cry silently, gaspingly, terribly.

"Helen's Song, man," singing, singing, "Helen's Song, man."

And the audience picks up the chant and holds hands and sways together.

I'm running around trying to keep order though I must admit I'm feeling rather Bill Grahamish and big over all the happenings in my space.

Neither garage nor studio is my space anymore but true lingual happening of sing-song unburdening.

"Helen's Song, man," singing, singing, "Helen's Song."

"And then where would we be now?" Walter stares up to the garage roof on his back and, half suppressing a godawful gasp, laughs.

He laughs on his back on the floor.

"Where would we be then, man?" He gets up on one knee and faces the audience, slowly rising, slowing holding out the sweater to them which has smothered him in its sweet-smelling presence.

"Helen's Song, man," singing, singing "Helen's Song."

"And how 'bout that other Helen, ese?" someone calls from the audience.

Peering down into the faces, Walter sees a storm-ravaged chola's face appealing to him now.

He calls out and forth and to anyone who will listen.

"Helen's Song, man," singing, singing, "Helen's Song."

He steps among the wires on stage past Carlos Santana with a beatific smile on his face dishing his latest to us in handfuls.

Walter stops and bows his head.

"Helen's Song, man," singing, singing, "Helen's Song."

And behind him the two Wetbacks Extempore leap to the mikes again.

They pounce into the song.

"Helen's Song, man," singing, singing, "Helen's Song."

The audience claps and sways.

Walter stands at the lip of the slightly raised stage built by me on a boring and sunny Saturday when I had only two acts to boast of, and asks, "What about the question, man, what about the question?"

"Say what?" they call back in the audience.

"What's gonna happen to us here people if we forget about la Helen?"

"Helen's Song, man," singing, singing, "Helen's Song."

And Carlos Santana rips forth with an ear-splitting guitar lick on his Stratomaster white Fender guitar lost in the heavens which are hidden by the rotten and decomposed ceiling letting in small bars of light this crazy evening.

He gets down.

And everybody follows his lead and gets down.

On one knee they bow their heads.

"Helen's Song, man," singing, singing, "Helen's Song."

And then Walter commands, "Everybody rise," and everybody rises.

Everybody sways on their feet.

A soft chant grows.

"Helen's Song, man," singing, singing, "Helen's Song."

"If we forget her we forget everything, we lose our souls."

"Helen's Song, man," singing, singing, "Helen's Song, man."

And then Helen la atira chola de Fresno comes forward from the wings.

She comes forward with a shyness diluted by Walter's

extended hand meeting her halfway across the stage.

"Helen's Song, man," singing, singing, "Helen's Song," rises omnivorously and gently.

The audience sways.

The band plays.

Santana informs.

Walter and la Helen de las calles en Fresno hug on stage.

Helen de so many years back in Walter's life stands to the side.

And they all look at each other and laugh.

"Helen's Song, man," singing, singing, "Helen's Song."

"Yeah, I remember you, ese," Helen Number Two speaks.

The old chola grabs the mike and casts her head down in embarrassment but truth. "I remember you, ese."

"Helen's Song, man," singing, singing, "Helen's Song."

"It was so many years ago." Walter raises his hand in one all-absolving gesture to the heavens.

Big, hardy tears flow steadily and unimpededly down his cheeks.

"That I saw you," he can't stop now, "outside the Safeway in Fresno, California."

"I smelled like sex, didn't I, ay?"

"Helen's Song, man," singing, singing, "Helen's Song, man."

And the people are chanting and swaying and filled with a happiness they've never felt before.

They need to be filled tonight.

A miracle is within my means.

Something big that I've never done before can happen here tonight.

It would take courage and a certain sangfroid attitude of hell-bent recklessness and giving compassion.

But it could be done.

It could be done.

Santana looks good on stage providing this wonderful background.

The Wetbacks round him off.

La Helen de Fresno clutches her mike with more confidence now.

Helen Number One (of the innocent times of Walter's youth) stands somberly by the two of them now.

"Helen's Song, man," singing, singing, "Helen's Song."

"You were there standing outside the Safeway, kind of in a hurry I think to buy something and go home."

"Helen's Song, man," singing, singing, "Helen's Song."

"It was a strange and terrible night," Walter lifts his hand to the heavens blocked by the roof again.

Outside is night and day and time unstoppered in an endless flow into my garage-studio choreographed by Santana floating now above the stage playing the guitar on his back.

La Helen de Fresno watches him and smiles in appreciation.

"Carlos, you always made me cry, man, in the old days."

He nods his head, eyes closed, hearing her voice through the chords he's licking.

"And you stood outside the Safeway in a real hurry to go in or something."

"Helen's Song, man," singing, singing, "Helen's Song."

"This is a song about redemption." Walter hurriedly paces the stage, addressing the audience who will hear him beyond her.

A microphone held in his hand trembles.

"It's about goodness and recognizing your sweet-smelling sex. . . ."

"You dissed me."

"Was not sin but . . ."

"I asked you for the time and you couldn't even give me the fucking time."

"Helen's Song, man," singing, singing, "Helen's Song."

"You walked by me like you were some big shit or something."

"Helen's Song, man," singing, singing, "Helen's Song,

man," grows louder and forceful.

Unspoken demands well up from the audience.

The two Wetbacks Extempore are in perfect tune with Santana.

Slowly, their native garb has been dissolved for their true native garb.

They wear the costumes of Mexico walking across the stage playing the ancient instruments of the people.

Santana smiles on his bed of clouds floating in the air above them.

They pass most holy herbs among each other in bouncing leaps across time and space.

Walter, caught up in a mist of past and present, begins to take his clothes off.

"Helen's Song, man," singing, singing, "Helen's Song."

He emits one frightful yell from his breast. "I never wanted to do anything bad! I loved my people! I really did!" and stretches out on the floor to be eaten.

"Helen's Song, man," singing, singing, "Helen's Song."

And slowly the people pass by him placing hands upon his breast.

The song fades out and finally ends. "Helen's Song, man," singing, singing, "Helen's Song," no more.

"Helen's Song, man," singing, singing, "Helen's Song."

Lionel G. Garcia

The Frying Pan

The man opened the old, heavy, wooden door and looked out into the night. He placed his hand over his eyes to shield his vision from the street lamp at the corner. It was the fog. Below him were the steps, five of them, and then the hard ground. He noticed the change, the cold Texas weather. Thirty minutes ago he had come to the door to help someone out, to keep them from falling down the steps, and he remembered clearly seeing the street light. Now he saw the bright light exaggerated through the beads of fog at what appeared to be a very short distance, as if he could have reached out from the door and touched the huge fire ball. Just then a strong gust of wind blew cold. Several sheets of newspaper tumbled and crackled in the wind in the street and went past to lodge with a snap at the bottom strand of barbed wire fence across the street. He heard the frightened dog from next door howl at the sounds the wind was making. He yelled at the dog to keep quiet because he knew every time a dog cried out someone would die. The dog heard him and stopped. He felt colder. He shuddered.

"Do you think it will snow?" Tomás asked. He was putting on his coat and hat, getting ready. He was the last one to leave.

"It's too cold to snow," said the man sticking his head out through the door and looking around but with the fog rolling in he could see nothing but the light. He closed the door tightly and then shook it several times. "It's as dark as the mouth of a wolf," he said coming back to the kerosene stove in the middle of the room. He rubbed his hands over the stove and then looked for his gloves which he could never seem to find. This time he found them in the right back pocket and he put them on. He turned around and warmed his backside. "No," he said, without being asked, "it's too cold to snow. They say that for it to snow it has to be warm. The warm air meets the cold air somewhere in the sky

193

and forms snow. Anyway that's what my father always used to say. It never snowed. And we always asked . . . and he always said the same thing: 'It's too cold to snow.'"

"Well," said Tomás with his coat and hat and gloves on, "it's time for me to go. I work tomorrow, you know."

"Since when do you work on Saturdays?"

"Since when? Since Benito put me on Saturdays."

"What a no-good, son of . . ."

"You don't have to say it. We all know what he is. And after all these years. Twenty five years I've worked for the highway."

"It's a shame," said the man shaking his head.

"You would think I would not have to do these things . . . like Saturday work. You would think . . ."

"Why didn't they promote you? Make you the foreman?" the man said, egging Tomás on.

"Well, I didn't expect that much," said Tomás. "I knew they would never give it to me. But why Benito? Of all people."

"I would be bitter, Tomás. So bitter. I don't know how I could work there."

"How can I quit? With four grown daughters and a wife? That is impossible. There comes a time when a man has to swallow his pride."

The man felt the warmth of the stove. He had his back to Tomás. He said, looking at the plain wall in front of him, "You have never been able to marry your daughters off."

"No," said Tomás. "I have not been lucky in that respect. Cenobia wants them around. Likes to keep them close to her. Most unusual but what can I say? I'm only the father."

"You could have asked for work at the courthouse."

"What do you mean? You know I tried. Everyone knows I tried."

"The word out," said the man, "was that you begged for work."

"I did," said Tomás, lowering his eyes. "I admit I begged. I have never lied about it."

"I'm glad this has come up between the two of us. I have wanted to ask you about it but I didn't know how to approach the subject. We were all surprised."

"You were surprised? Think of how we all on the crew felt. When the engineer from Austin came that day and stayed for a week we knew there was something wrong."

"Didn't you think," the man said, turning to warm his front and rubbing his gloves over the stove, "that you would be the one? You had been there for so long. Benito had only been there for a short time . . ."

"Two years. That's how long he had been there. But look at Manuel. He had been there eighteen years. Alfredo twenty. Bustos twenty two. These are smart men. Not like me."

"You're as smart as the next man," the man said. He had been moving around the stove to find the most heat and was by Tomás.

"No," said Tomás. "I can't read or write."

"I thought you could read and write."

"No. I never went to school."

"That doesn't make any difference. I would be the most bitter man in the world," the man said so resolutely that it caused a spear of pain to penetrate Tomás' heart.

"I have my job to do and that is all. I do it well. You ask . . ."

"I know. I don't have to ask. And not to be bitter? Why, that's another story."

"So now they put me to work on Saturdays and the newer men . . . men who have not been there ten years . . . they get off on Saturdays. To be with their families. To be able to get out and drink. What do you think?"

"I've said it before and I'll say it again. I would be bitter. You just ask my friends and see if I haven't said that. When someone asks me why you're not bitter then I say that I don't know. I don't know how a man treated like you have been treated could possibly not be bitter with his work, his boss, his life."

"You've said quite a bit there," said Tomás. "You have talked about me?"

"Oh, yes," said the man. "Many times. Not to insult you, you understand. But to talk about how cruel life is some times. You are the perfect example of how life doesn't deal fairly with people. In that respect we have talked about you."

"I appreciate that," said Tomás. He was working his way to the door.

"Benito never forgave you. Is that what this is all about?"

Tomás stopped and began to walk toward the man. He approached the stove and warmed his gloves. It was a stern look he gave the man. "I would appreciate it if you would retract that statement," he said.

"With all due respects," said the man. He had felt threatened for that instant when Tomás had approached him. Now Tomás appeared cooled down.

The man took no chances with drunks. He went around to stand across the stove from Tomás. He said, "Why wouldn't Benito forgive you? Let things go. Why this bitterness toward you for such a long time?"

"I have pride in my family," said Tomás. "Maybe I had too much pride but who is to decide that? You?"

"No," said the man quickly. "I would never presume to tell you how much pride a man should have."

"You see how difficult it is? Life is not simple, my friend. You just don't say to a man why don't you do this or that. There are many answers and more questions than answers . . . or more answers than questions."

"Still, your daughter . . ."

The remark sobered Tomás instantly. He said, "My daughter is not in this thing. She never was. Benito may have had certain feelings. But I can assure you my daughter was never in this thing." Tomás felt hot and he took off his hat and gloves. He said, "I suppose some other man might have treated this differently. But I surely didn't."

The man said, "I am not familiar . . ."

"No, sir," said Tomás, "life is not simple. When the engineer gathered us up and said that he had been talking to Austin all the week we knew there was trouble. Then he made the announcement that Benito would be the foreman and we all applauded like we were supposed to. But you could see it in the faces of all the men. The disappointment. Then their thoughts turned to me and they were all staring at me. Feeling sorry for me."

"It's been hell," said the man.

"It's been more than hell," said Tomás.

"I could not have lived through the bitterness," said the man. "I'm sorry but I have to say it. And everyone agrees with me."

Tomás said, "Too bad so few came tonight. Tonight was the perfect night to drink."

The man had turned his backside to the stove. He turned his head and looked over his shoulder and said, "It's getting too cold for some of them."

"And here I was waiting," said Tomás. "Waiting for friends, for snow."

"We had good company," said the man. His name was Arturo and his family lived in a ranch outside of town where they raised cheap calves from inferior cows. He had two brothers, one who worked at the jail and one who was in jail. He had gone behind the counter and opened the wooden box. He took the money that was in it and placed it inside his coat pocket. "And I hope I was company to you."

"You were," said Tomás. "I enjoyed myself. Especially that story about the coyote."

"Oh, yes," remembered the man. "The coyote is a very smart animal."

"Smarter than man," said Tomás with such certainty that they both had nothing else to say about the subject.

The man was turning off the lights, hoping Tomás would not bring up the coyote story again because if he did then Arturo knew that for sure Tomás would go on to the story of the snakes and then the fox and then the deer, and then who knew? It was better not to lead Tomás into anything. He wanted to hum a tune to stop Tomás but he refused to hum at that late hour. Humming, he thought, was for the morning hours. Tomás was standing at the door ready to leave. He had put his hat and gloves back on. The man could see Tomás' silhouette swaying across the threshold. "You're not drunk, Tomás? Are you?" he asked, turning off the beer sign.

"Oh, no," said Tomás. "I never get drunk . . . It sure is cold. When did it turn so cold?"

"Just a minute ago," said the man. He turned off the kerosene stove and waited for a while for it to pop. He waited. "It's foggy too," he said.

Tomás adjusted his hat, pushed it farther down his head. He said, "When did it get so foggy?"

The stove popped. It was off. The man touched it with his bare hands and felt the heat. He reached for his gloves in his right back pocket and they were not there. He searched and found them in his coat pocket. He walked to the door and remembered he had to get his keys out so he took off only his right glove and found his keys. Tomás was standing on the top step, teetering.

The man was locking the door. He said, "I'm glad we had the conversation. It was something that needed to be said. By me, I mean."

Tomás was holding tight with both hands on the door frame. He said, "I know everyone makes fun of me but I am not bitter, if that is what you want me to say."

"Oh, no." said Arturo. "Some of us are bitter and some of us are not. Some of us have cause to be bitter. Some of us have not."

"And you believe that I should be bitter?" said Tomás.

Arturo said, "Yes. I believe it as much as I believe that there is a God in Heaven."

When he finished locking the door he banged on it. He then

tried to open it and finally satisfied himself that the door was locked. Then he worried about the stove and unlocked the door and went back inside, took the glove from his left hand off and felt the stove. He knelt down and looked into the burner and it was off. He kicked the stove and heard it pop again. He came back and locked the door. "I can't remember anymore," he said. "Last night I had to come back at three in the morning to make sure I had locked the door. You know what?"

"What?" asked Tomás.

"I had locked it. It's that Margarita awoke me and asked me, 'Are you sure you locked the door?' and then I couldn't sleep thinking about it. You know how it is."

All this time Tomás had waited for him at the top step, clinging to the door frame. The man locked the door again, kicked it and tried to force it open.

"It's locked," said Tomás. "Can't you see?"

"Did you see me lock it?"

"Yes. I saw you lock it."

"And the stove? Did you see me turn it off?"

"You turned it off," said Tomás, shivering in the cold.

"So tonight," said Arturo to himself, "when I'm in bed asleep and Margarita wakes me up and asks me about the door then I can say I locked it and I can be sure I locked it . . . You saw me lock it, didn't you?"

"Yes," said Tomás, pressing with his two fingers on his lower lids, "with these eyes I saw it."

Tomás could not see his hand in the fog. He looked about for some reference point and could only see the brightness of the street lamp at the corner. He headed in that direction and he stepped on his own foot and fell the rest of the way to the hard ground.

"Mother of Mercy," he cried out. "What happened to me?"

Arturo had been messing with the door and he came quickly to try to get Tomás up. Arturo said, "What happened? How did you fall?"

"I stepped on my foot," said Tomás. "What luck. But I am not hurt."

"Are you sure?"

"Yes," said Tomás. "If you give me room I can get up by myself."

Arturo said, "I told you you were drunk."

"I have never been drunk in my life," Tomás said. "Help me up."

"I am trying to help you up," Arturo said. "Thank God you're not heavy. I thought you said you could get up by yourself."

"I can," Tomás said, "but since you are here I might as well take advantage."

Arturo stood Tomás up and turned him toward the street lamp. "That is the direction you take," he said, pointing.

Tomás said, "My dear friend. To show you how much I think of you I would like to invite you to come eat with me tonight."

"It's late, Tomás," Arturo said. "Maybe some other time. When it's earlier. Then maybe I will go. Don't think I don't appreciate the invitation. But look at your poor wife. We are not going to disturb her at this hour."

"She doesn't mind," Tomás said. "You can bet it won't be the first time I wake her up to fix me something to eat. And it won't be the last time."

"No," said the man, "I wouldn't want to impose on your wife."

"My good man," said Tomás, "that is what wives are for."

"Not mine," said Arturo. He turned to his left and walked off. "Good night and be careful," he said.

Tomás looked around and Arturo had disappeared into the fog. He could only hear Arturo's slowly fading footsteps crunching in the limestone. He turned himself around to face the street lamp and began to walk slowly home. "To the street lamp," he muttered to himself.

Lionel G. Garcia

* * *

He was under the street lamp. He walked around the pole
looking up at the light and became disoriented for a while until
he saw the lights from the grocery store across the street. Now he
knew where he was. He crossed the street and went to the front
of the store. At the window he saw the few fruits and vegetables
Mr. Garcia was selling. The night light was on and he looked
inside to where the meat market was. All the sights made him
even hungrier. Tomorrow he would buy a chicken and have his
wife roast it with potatoes and onions and garlic and . . . He
could not think of anything else. He could not think of the name
for the long orange vegetable that grew underground. He gave
up. Then he wanted bread and crackers with butter and corn bread.
Corn bread! He had not had corn bread in a long time. Cenobia
had not baked corn bread since God knew when. He could smell
flour tortillas cooking on a griddle somewhere, the beautiful smell
of fresh bread carried to him in each bead of fog. A few steps
later and he could smell *chorizo* frying, hot pork and chili pep-
pers heated to a crisp. He felt like chewing on the fog. And then
there was coffee. If it had been up to him there would be potatoes
frying in the *chorizo* grease and then he would add the eggs.
What a beautiful mixture. The aroma drove him toward the house.

He heard a voice coming from behind, from the vicinity
of the tavern, and he went back to see who it was. Perhaps some
friend in need. In the fog at the top of the steps was Arturo having come back to make sure he had locked the door.

"You must go eat with me," said Tomás. "Flour tortillas,
chorizo, potatoes, and eggs with coffee."

Arturo said, "Your wife would kill us."

"Cenobia," said Tomás, "is the perfect lady. She enjoys
cooking for me and my friends."

"No one," said Arturo, "enjoys cooking for you and your
friends at this hour. It is time to go home. You have to work
tomorrow."

201

"Yes, I do," said Tomás. "Have to work tomorrow. Or is it today?"

"Today," said Arturo. "It is already today."

"And you are sure you don't want to go with me to eat at my house? As my guest?"

Arturo pushed on the door and said, "No. I have to go home. Margarita is worried by now about me . . . You did see me lock the door, didn't you?"

"With these two eyes," said Tomás.

Arturo thought for a second and unlocked the door. He said, "I don't remember if I turned off the stove."

"You did," said Tomás. "I saw you. You turned off the stove and then you locked the door and then you unlocked the door and went to turn off the stove again and then you locked the door again. And here you are now unlocking the door to check on the stove."

"One more time and that is all," announced Arturo. He opened the door and said, "Was the door open? Or did I unlock it?"

"You unlocked it," said Tomás. "Just right now you unlocked it."

"That's a relief to know," Arturo said.

Arturo went inside and in the darkness checked to make sure the stove was off. On the way back he tripped over a chair and fell moaning.

"God, what has happened to me?" he cried out.

Tomás went in to try and find him in the dark but could not. Instead, he tripped over another chair and fell also. He cried out when he hit the floor and Arturo found him by the noise he made trying to get up. He helped Tomás and they went out holding on to each other.

Arturo locked the door. He gave the door a few shoves with his shoulder while twisting the knob. "There," he said, "the door is locked. I saw it with my own eyes."

Tomás had jumped off the threshold and was standing on the ground. He had not wanted to fall off the steps. He watched as Arturo came down the steps and said, "You refuse then to eat with me tonight."

"Yes," said Arturo. "I am going to bed. The door is locked and the stove is off."

Tomás stood alone as he heard Arturo's crunching footsteps fade into the night. Then he buttoned his coat to the throat and turned and headed for the street light. At the corner he followed his way to the grocery store. He would be sure to buy that chicken tomorrow and Cenobia would roast it with potatoes, and onions, and whatever the name was for that long orange vegetable that grows underground. A few steps later and as if by magic the smells of tortillas and *chorizo* and coffee reached him. The smells engulfed him for a block. At the highway he felt the gust of cold wind whipping at his pants, numbing his legs. He held on to his hat and turned right and crossed over to the sidewalk. It was windier on that side and he was having trouble with his legs. After a while he crossed the bridge and only one car crossed while he was on it. He tried to flag the car down but the driver did not see him. Perhaps a friend that could take him home. Far ahead he could see the glitter of the street light. One by one, from street light to street light, he walked until he saw the dirt road off the highway and he turned left, went a block and turned left again. His dog began to bark at the strange apparition coming toward the house at this hour. The dog had forgotten that he had not put Tomás to bed. When he smelled Tomás on the street he quieted down and went back to sleep.

The house was dark and Tomás could not see well. He tried going up the porch stairs but he could not. With his legs so numb he kept inching backwards on the first step. He decided to climb the porch to one side of the stairs. He rolled on the porch and got up with the help of the old iron chair. He opened the door and walked in. He turned on the lights in the kitchen and put his hat on top of the refrigerator. The house felt warm. Cenobia had left the four burners on the stove lit. He found eggs and *chorizo* and tortillas in the refrigerator. He looked in the oven and found the old frying pan, the one with the jagged handle, the one he had told them over and over to throw away, and he placed it on the fire. He opened the package of *chorizo* and tore a large pinch off and threw it on the frying pan. The smell immediately caught his senses and he was back one block off the grocery store. He turned up the fire on the stove. The question crossing his mind was whether he wanted to have potatoes. He thought about it for a while and then he remembered that the vegetable he was thinking about at the grocery store was the carrot. The carrot. Strange how sometimes he could not remember. He decided against potatoes. It was too much trouble. He wanted the meal quickly so he turned the fire up some more. The *chorizo* was jumping in the frying pan. He added two eggs and he put a tortilla on another burner to warm.

He had some coffee left over from this morning and he took a cup, poured the coffee into the cup and placed it directly on another burner. But the cup was not level and the coffee spilled on the burner, snuffing it out. He quickly turned the burner off. The spilled coffee had filled the pan under the burner. He tried to pick up the burner to clean it and he burned his fingers. The *chorizo* and eggs took on a special aroma, the smell of burning pork fat. Quickly, when he realized what was going on, he turned off the burner but by now the grease had caught fire. Smoke began to cover the whole kitchen. He ran to the dining room and snatched the tablecloth, knocking down the glass candy dish and the glass figurines the daughters collected. All of the glassware fell to the floor and broke. He flung the tablecloth like a fishnet over the burning grease. That extinguished the flame but when he tried to yank the tablecloth off, it had gotten stuck to the jagged handle of the frying pan, and he brought the hot frying pan and grease and *chorizo* and egg on top of his head. He let out a scream and then he realized he would wake up the whole house. The *chorizo* and eggs he had longed for had rolled off his head and were on the floor, stepped on while he was trying to get the tablecloth and the hot frying pan off him. He felt better. He was not burned badly. He slipped on the food on the floor while trying to untangle himself from the tablecloth and fell, hitting the back of his head on the door jam. He must have lain on the floor for a while. When he awoke, the whole kitchen and the dining room were full of smoke.

He went into the tiny living room and sat down in the old stuffed armchair where he felt the familiar, loose iron spring poke him on his left back side. On his right was the old sofa which Cenobia had upholstered badly in pink felt. Cenobia had left the gas heater on and the flames flickered against the burning asbestos on its little fire wall. He could hear the wind sing through the house, mixed with Cenobia's snoring in the next room. His daughters were asleep at the end of the hallway. Underneath the house he could hear the dog growling at the smoke seeping down from the cracks on the floor. He stared into the flame of the heater which made little wisps of fire in the asbestos and could see Benito and the engineer from Austin and Arturo and all the men. He crossed his leg and on the tip of his boot he saw a glob of *chorizo* and egg. He watched the glob slide down the boot to the floor. What a simple act it was to watch the glob slide down his boot but what complex waves of emotions it brought out in him. He was finally enraged.

He ran into the kitchen and found the frying pan on the floor and began to stomp on it. Then he kicked it against the kitchen door which led outside. He opened the door and kicked the frying pan out into the backyard. This was not enough. He followed the frying pan out and placed it on the log he used for killing goats and he went into the garage and came out with the axe. He raised the axe over his head and swung down on the frying pan with all his might. The axe went through the frying pan and stuck into the log where he had the hardest time trying to dislodge it. When he finally did unstick the axe, he found that it was embedded in the frying pan. He had to straddle the frying pan and rock the axe handle back and forth, back and forth, to free it. He picked up the frying pan and set it on the log again.

This time the blow from the axe separated the frying pan into two equal parts. Unfortunately, one of the parts flew right into his shin and in the cold the pain was multiplied many times and he fell to the ground holding his leg. He raised his trouser leg up and he could see the blood coming from the cut. He figured that his trousers were torn and he examined the leg and he was right. There was a small tear where the metal had gone through to cut his leg. These were his going-out pants. It angered him so much, made him so much more angrier, that he found the two pieces of frying pan and he stacked them on the log and delivered to them the heaviest axe blow of the night. The force was such that he melded the two pieces of frying pan to the axe and he could not take the pieces off the axe no matter what he tried. He used a hammer. He tried the sledge hammer. He tried a screwdriver and when he tried to wedge it between the axe and the frying pan the screwdriver flew off and cut his hand. He tried putting the axe in the fork of the tree next to the log and swung on the axe handle but all that did was dig the axe and the pieces of frying pan into the tree. Now the axe was stuck inside the fork. He studied the problem for a while and then his perspiration turned cold and he had to go in to warm up.

He was sitting on the armchair in the living room feeling the loose coil on his backside, staring at the flame in the heater, when the thought came to him. He got up and went into the bedroom where Cenobia was snoring. He looked inside the closet and found his shot gun. He took it and got the shells from the dresser drawer and stepped out loading the shotgun as he went. When he got to the log he took aim and he began to shoot the frying pan off the axe while it rested on the fork of the tree.

Cenobia and the daughters were standing at the door watching him.

"What are you doing?" Cenobia shouted to him from the door.

"Killing the frying pan," he shouted back. "What else could you see me doing?"

Lionel G. Garcia

"Come inside. You're going to freeze to death. What a mess you've made," she said.

He had run out of shells and he sat down on the log with the hot shotgun on his lap. The axe was still lodged into the frying-pan pieces and it and the frying-pan pieces were lodged into the fork of the tree. The tree was badly wounded and would die the slow death of two years, a year after he had died. He felt the warmth of the blood trickling down his leg into his boot. His sock was heavy with blood. A heavy gust of wind blew and with it came the debris from the yard blown across his sight. The fingers he had burned on the stove began to hurt in a dull pain. He felt the mess in his hair and he remembered that it had been quite a while since he was outside without his hat.

The fog had cleared. The quarter moon was out, directly overhead. He heard Cenobia's rooster crow at the back of the yard in the hen house. The neighbor's rooster answered him from next door. He could see the millions of stars shining brightly. It would be way below freezing before daylight. It was too cold to snow.

Cenobia and the daughters had not been able to go back to sleep when they found the mess. After they cleaned up, Cenobia went to the door feeling sorry for him. She saw him sitting on the log, his shadows made coarse by the moonlight. He was smoking a cigarette which he had rolled. How many early mornings had she found him sitting out there alone? She walked out to the log and sat by him. She held his hand and said, "Come on in. You're going to freeze to death."

Tomás said, more to himself than to her, "Today, I'm not going to go to work."

"Oh," Cenobia said, "you always say that and you're the first one to rise."

"I'm going to buy a chicken for you to roast. I want potatoes and onions and carrots."

"Whatever you say," Cenobia said.

As he walked toward the house next to Cenobia he said,

207

"You don't know how much I have hated that old frying pan."

"Why?" she asked, looking at him.

"I don't know," he replied.

"Well now it's gone," said Cenobia.

"I feel better now," Tomás said.

Omar Castañeda

Chapter 21 - Excerpt from *Islas Coloradas*

"You know," Karen says, "I really do appreciate everything you've done."

"Nothing," Amelia replies. She waves it off.

Karen and Amelia sit beside each other. Across the aisle, Sam and Boy sit close together, resting against each other. Whatever doubt Karen might have kept over Sam and Boy being lovers has long ago disappeared. She is glad that the hoopla over Gary's disappearance has made dealing with that easier. Back at home, she might have had trouble knowing what to think or feel. She would have gone in the direction of her context. Here, searching for Gary, already in a mode of "foreign-ness," she can slip into the simple choice of it. Or rather the simple truth of it, uncomplicated except for the tonnage of preconceptions and automatic and conditioned responses that would rear their bigoted heads back home. Here, in Islas Coloradas, with everything displaced for Karen and with the whole country itself seeking to come free of something ingrained, something false and unhealthy, Sam's revolution seems wholly pious, if nothing else because of its clarity. Its uncluttered frankness makes it parsimonious, sublime.

All of this works through Karen's mind as they settle into the small plane and push back for the one-hour trip. And all of this works its inevitable way to the subject of Amelia and her possible relationship with Gary. If she can accept another kind of relationship for Sam—though "accept" is not right, so condescending—she could accept something different with Gary. Perhaps. She watches Amelia out of the corner of her eye for the first half hour. They are all caught up in the excitement of the search, but within minutes the first lull comes upon them all. She observes Amelia. She takes careful note of Amelia's potent sensuality. It is not a sensuality that Karen has experienced in America. It isn't the type aired in magazines and film. American sensuality is either ominous—dangerous and full of threat—or too traditional—like farm girls or college girls who have bought the entire, established scheme of things. The first has everything of the power of lust and all of its decadence. The second is mindless, clean, doomed to perpetuate the entire sexist world in ordered fashion. The first, pitbull tied to the master's post, the second is the dog in the house, speaking as ordered; rolling as prescribed; made up to naturalize the world of masculine economy and virile religiosity.

But Amelia is something else entirely. Something so different for Karen that she knows she does not come near understanding it. All she can do is take pot-shots at it, hoping to get a glimmer of it as it peers out in its random way, as it occasionally manifests itself to be more namable than when it is just a steady and constant electricity about her. Hot sexuality is part of it. Yet the violence of that heat is pure, not tainted. Earnestness is part of it, but with a pristine uninhibitedness. A flexibility of limb is an element as well, but it is a flexibility that speaks of freedom of mind, as well. It is a curious mixture of intelligence—which in her case is inextricably bound to her sexuality—and an innocence that knows the pleasures of the body without the tight ligaments of mind. Somehow, the core of this sensuality is centered in the muscles of her abdomen. Karen knows that if she could have eyes to see auras, she would see vibrant colors emanating from Amelia's abdomen. A muscled, but rounded belly.

So what if she has slept with Gary? In a fleeting vision, Karen imagines that she would have slept with the woman too, and tags at the end of the vision the defensive clause, "if she were a man." Her mind creates the image to truly recognize her attraction to Amelia; the clause is simply language in vision, the conditioned, the artifice. What she reckons with is a desired meeting-up with this essence she wishes she possessed and in this meeting she is not a woman or a man, but both at once, some amorphous melding that is forever non-existent except in the back

Omar Castañeda

reaches of a mind where infinite possibilities unfold without the
social invention of desire and the overly simple male/female.

Sitting beside her, their legs barely touching, both thinking predominantly about Gary, Karen lets go whatever jealousy
she first acquired and what images of flesh that may have ini-
tially disturbed her. This is a woman she wishes she was, in part.
She does not diminish her own education and brand of life, but
there is yet some puzzle of womanhood that this woman has
solved and that Karen has yet to solve. It does not occur to her
how it may be linked to race and power. She is too American for
that. Instead, when this letting go happens on the plane, it leaves
behind an honest appreciation for Amelia's selflessness. "You
know," Karen says again, "I really do appreciate everything
you've done."

Amelia turns. These two women see into each other, now
that Karen allows entry. They make a certain peace, with words a
small portal to some place more meaningful than language.

"Gracias," Amelia says.

Between them, it is not a word, but a meaningful low
growl and sibilant that is a shiver for them both. A shared and
mutual shiver.

Miguel Arteta

Nov 19

Finished shooting Star Maps. I lack energy.
I have to get a job. The responsibility thing has been over me
like nothin' forever. When is the big change gonna come. I say
don't throw your power away, and is that good? And I feel bad
that I just can't talk and talk
like Michael White.

Always looking for family. Wow!
And sex, what about it, is Sam Fuller
right, "Maybe there's a heaven w/ lots of
girls in bikinies waiting, but I don't
think so." Be, say it.
I'm going crazy, You got to learn.